THE MAGIC LANTERN

THE MAGIC LANTERN

HAVING A BALL AND CHRISTMAS EVE

A Novel and Novella by
JOSÉ TOMÁS DE CUÉLLAR

Translated from the Spanish by
MARGARET CARSON

EDITED AND WITH AN INTRODUCTION
BY MARGO GLANTZ

OXFORD
UNIVERSITY PRESS

2000

OXFORD

UNIVERSITY PRESS

Oxford New York
Athens Auckland Bangkok Bogotá
Buenos Aires Calcutta Cape Town Chennai Dar es Salaam
Delhi Florence Hong Kong Istanbul Karachi
Kuala Lumpur Madrid Melbourne
Mexico City Mumbai Nairobi Paris São Paolo Singapore
Taipei Tokyo Toronto Warsaw

and associated companies in
Berlin Ibadan

Copyright © 2000 by Oxford University Press, Inc.

Published by Oxford University Press, Inc.
198 Madison Avenue, New York, New York 10016

Oxford is a registered trademark of Oxford University Press.

Library of Congress Cataloging-in-Publication Data
Cuéllar, José Tomás de, 1830–1894.
[La lintera mágica. English, Selections]
The magic lantern : a novel [*sic*] / by José Tomás de Cuéllar;
translated from the Spanish by Margaret Carson;
edited and with an introduction by Margo Glantz.
p. cm. — (Library of Latin America)
Contents: Having a ball — Christmas Eve.
ISBN 0-19-511503-1 — ISBN 0-19-511502-3
1. Cuéllar, José Tomás de, 1830–1894—Translations into English.
I. Carson, Margaret.   II. Glantz, Margo.
III. Cuéllar, José Tomás de, 1830–1894. Baile y cochino . . . English.
IV. Cuéllar, José Tomás de, 1830–1894. La Noche Buena. English.
V. Title.   VI. Series.
PQ7297.C77 A23 2000
863—dc21 99–059209

1 3 5 7 9 8 6 4 2

Printed in the United States of America
on acid-free paper

Contents

Series Editors'
General Introduction

The Library of Latin America series makes available in translation major nineteenth-century authors whose work has been neglected in the English-speaking world. The titles for the translations from the Spanish and Portuguese were suggested by an editorial committee that included Jean Franco (general editor responsible for works in Spanish), Richard Graham (series editor responsible for works in Portuguese), Tulio Halperín Donghi (at the University of California, Berkeley), Iván Jaksić (at the University of Notre Dame), Naomi Lindstrom (at the University of Texas at Austin), Francine Masiello (at the University of California, Berkeley), and Eduardo Lozano of the Library at the University of Pittsburgh. The late Antonio Cornejo Polar of the University of California, Berkeley, was also one of the founding members of the committee. The translations have been funded thanks to the generosity of the Lampadia Foundation and the Andrew W. Mellon Foundation.

During the period of national formation between 1810 and into the early years of the twentieth century, the new nations of Latin America fashioned their identities, drew up constitutions, engaged in bitter struggles over territory, and debated questions of education, government, ethnicity, and culture. This was a unique period unlike the process of nation formation in Europe and one which should be more familiar than it is to students of comparative politics, history, and literature.

The image of the nation was envisioned by the lettered classes—a minority in countries in which indigenous, mestizo, black, or mulatto peasants and slaves predominated—although there were also alternative nationalisms at the grassroots level. The cultural elite were well educated in European thought and letters, but as statesmen, journalists, poets, and academics, they confronted the problem of the racial and linguistic heterogeneity of the continent and the difficulties of integrating the population into a modern nation-state. Some of the writers whose works will be translated in the Library of Latin America series played leading roles in politics. Fray Servando Teresa de Mier, a friar who translated Rousseau's *The Social Contract* and was one of the most colorful characters of the independence period, was faced with imprisonment and expulsion from Mexico for his heterodox beliefs; on his return, after independence, he was elected to the congress. Domingo Faustino Sarmiento, exiled from his native Argentina under the presidency of Rosas, wrote *Facundo: Civilización y barbarie*, a stinging denunciation of that government. He returned after Rosas' overthrow and was elected president in 1868. Andrés Bello was born in Venezuela, lived in London where he published poetry during the independence period, settled in Chile where he founded the University, wrote his grammar of the Spanish language, and drew up the country's legal code.

These post-independence intelligentsia were not simply dreaming castles in the air, but vitally contributed to the founding of nations and the shaping of culture. The advantage of hindsight may make us aware of problems they themselves did not foresee, but this should not affect our assessment of their truly astonishing energies and achievements. It is still surprising that the writing of Andrés Bello, who contributed fundamental works to so many different fields, has never been translated into English. Although there is a recent translation of Sarmiento's celebrated *Facundo*, there is no translation of his memoirs, *Recuerdos de provincia (Provincial Recollections)*. The predominance of memoirs in the Library of Latin America series is no accident—many of these offer entertaining insights into a vast and complex continent.

Nor have we neglected the novel. The series includes new translations of the outstanding Brazilian writer Joaquim Maria Machado de Assis' work, including *Dom Casmurro* and *The Posthumous Memoirs of Brás Cubas*. There is no reason why other novels and writers who are not so well known outside Latin America—the Peruvian novelist Clorinda Matto de Turner's *Aves sin nido*, Nataniel Aguirre's *Juan de la Rosa*, José de

Alencar's *Iracema*, Juana Manuela Gorriti's short stories — should not be read with as much interest as the political novels of Anthony Trollope.

A series on nineteenth-century Latin America cannot, however, be limited to literary genres such as the novel, the poem, and the short story. The literature of independent Latin America was eclectic and strongly influenced by the periodical press newly liberated from scrutiny by colonial authorities and the Inquisition. Newspapers were miscellanies of fiction, essays, poems, and translations from all manners of European writing. The novels written on the eve of Mexican Independence by José Joaquín Fernández de Lizardi included disquisitions on secular education and law, and denunciations of the evils of gaming and idleness. Other works, such as a well-known poem by Andrés Bello, "Ode to Tropical Agriculture," and novels such as *Amalia* by José Mármol and the Bolivian Nataniel Aguirre's *Juan de la Rosa*, were openly partisan. By the end of the century, sophisticated scholars were beginning to address the history of their countries, as did João Capistrano de Abreu in his *Capítulos de história colonial*.

It is often in memoirs such as those by Fray Servando Teresa de Mier or Sarmiento that we find the descriptions of everyday life that in Europe were incorporated into the realist novel. Latin American literature at this time was seen largely as a pedagogical tool, a "light" alternative to speeches, sermons, and philosophical tracts—though, in fact, especially in the early part of the century, even the readership for novels was quite small because of the high rate of illiteracy. Nevertheless, the vigorous orally transmitted culture of the gaucho and the urban underclasses became the linguistic repertoire of some of the most interesting nineteenth-century writers—most notably José Hernández, author of the "gauchesque" poem "Martín Fierro," which enjoyed an unparalleled popularity. But for many writers the task was not to appropriate popular language but to civilize, and their literary works were strongly influenced by the high style of political oratory.

The editorial committee has not attempted to limit its selection to the better-known writers such as Machado de Assis; it has also selected many works that have never appeared in translation or writers whose work has not been translated recently. The series now makes these works available to the English-speaking public.

Because of the preferences of funding organizations, the series initially focuses on writing from Brazil, the Southern Cone, the Andean region, and Mexico. Each of our editions will have an introduction that places the work in its appropriate context and includes explanatory notes.

We owe special thanks to Robert Glynn of the Lampadia Foundation, whose initiative gave the project a jump start, and to Richard Ekman of the Andrew W. Mellon Foundation, which also generously supported the project. We also thank the Rockefeller Foundation for funding the 1996 symposium "Culture and Nation in Iberoamerica," organized by the editorial board of the Library of Latin America. We received substantial institutional support and personal encouragement from the Institute of Latin American Studies of the University of Texas at Austin. The support of Edward Barry of Oxford University Press has been crucial, as has the advice and help of Ellen Chodosh of Oxford University Press. The first volumes of the series were published after the untimely death, on July 3, 1997, of Maria C. Bulle, who, as an associate of the Lampadia Foundation, supported the idea from its beginning.

—Jean Franco
—Richard Graham

Introduction

José Tomás de Cuéllar was born in Mexico City in 1830, a few years after Mexico won its independence from Spain in 1821. His life spanned an era of intense changes, economic and military setbacks, and diverse and short-lived forms of government: the brief episode of Empire headed by Agustín de Iturbide, followed by the Republic, whose first president was José Guadalupe Victoria. During this time the debates about centralism versus federalism began, resulting in clashes between Conservatives and Liberals, and battles between rival Masonic lodges (Scottish and York). The outcome was anarchy, which prepared the way for the numerous and catastrophic appearances of Antonio López de Santa Anna on the Mexican political scene, and the loss of an important part of the national territory in the aftermath of the War of Texas and the American invasion. Cuéllar, as a cadet in the Colegio Militar, took part in the defense of Mexico City against the invading army in 1847; after this defeat, disillusioned, he abandoned his military career and entered the Academia de San Carlos. He studied painting without much success, then took up photography, a pursuit that would later be useful to him in sketching the characters that wander through his *Magic Lantern* series. Significantly, *Christmas Eve* has the subtitle "Negatives Exposed from December 24th to 25th, 1882."

Cuéllar began his literary career by writing poetry, and by 1850 was contributing to *Seminario de las señoritas* and *Ilustración Mexicana*. He then turned to the stage, somewhat successfully, writing plays that have completely lost their meaning today: *El viejecito Chacón* [The Old Man, Chacón], *¡Qué lástima de muchachos!* [Those Poor Boys!], and a patriotic satire directed against Mexican francophiles, *Natural y figura* [From the Cradle to the Grave]. In 1869, after the French Intervention and the fall of the Empire of Maximilian (1863–1867), Cuéllar moved to San Luís Potosí and co-founded a weekly newspaper, *La Ilustración Potosina*, where his novel, *Ensalada de pollos* [A Sampler of Dandies], was first published. With this novel, Cuéllar initiated his famous series, which he called (imitating Balzac to a certain degree) *La linterna mágica* [The Magic Lantern]. He also published an unsuccessful historical novel set in eighteenth-century Mexico, *El pecado del siglo* [The Sin of the Century], which was similar to the serials Vicente Riva Palacio began to write in 1868. In 1871, after returning to the capital, Cuéllar (under his pen name, Facundo) published the first edition of his *Magic Lantern* series with the well-known printer, Ignacio Cumplido, which included a new version of *Ensalada de pollos* as well as *La historia de Chucho el Ninfo* [The Story of Chucho, the Playboy], *Isolina la ex-figurante* [Isolina, the Ex-Understudy], *Las jamonas* [Fashionable Matrons], *Las gentes que son así* [People Are Like That], and *Gabriel el cerrajero o las hijas de mi papá* [Gabriel, the Locksmith, or My Papa's Daughters]. Cuéllar contributed serial novels and sketches of everyday life and manners to the most important newspapers and magazines of his time: *La Ilustración Mexicana*, *El Siglo XIX*, *Las Cosquillas*, *El Eco del Comercio*, and *El Federalista*. The second edition of his *Magic Lantern* series, comprising twenty-four small volumes, was published in Spain from 1889 to 1892, with the first six volumes printed in Barcelona and the rest in Santander. This new edition reprinted all the novels published in the previous edition, and included three new texts: *Los marid-itos* [Little Husbands], *Los fuereños* [The Out-of-Towners], and *La Noche Buena* [Christmas Eve].

Like many other Liberal politicians and writers in Mexico, Cuéllar was both an actor in and spectator to a long series of catastrophes suffered by the country during the second half of the nineteenth century: the Wars of the Reform (1858–61), and the French Intervention and the Empire of Maximilian (1863–67), in addition to the vicissitudes of the Restored Republic (1867). After the death of President Benito Juárez in 1872, Cuéllar aligned himself with the government of Porfirio Díaz, the dictator who defined his administration with the slogan "Order and Progress." In his later years, Cuéllar received a meager compensation: he was given various diplomatic posts, first as a member of the Mexican delegation in Washington and then, in Mexico City, at the Ministry of Foreign Relations, where he held several midlevel positions. In 1894 he was named corresponding member to the Royal Academy of the Spanish Language. In that same year, on February 11, he died in Mexico City.

Literature and the Nation

Carlos Monsiváis has noted:

As an observer of manners, Cuéllar is chiefly influenced by the Spanish (Mariano José de Larra) and the French, and by the Mexicans [José Joaquín Fernández de] Lizardi, [Ignacio] Altamirano, and Guillermo Prieto. Cuéllar in turn is the precursor to Ángel de Campo *"Micrós"* and Emilio Rabasa. Like these writers, he moralizes incessantly, since that is his duty (to write is to preach) and because at that time, it was assumed that readers received these sermons with gratitude. A writer of manners was expected to record the most notorious ways of life and reprimand them. By issuing these reprimands, he contributed to the code of permissible behavior in a society that was by now partly secular, or at least sufficiently liberated from clerical power so as not to rely on the formal and, in the majority of cases, on the spiritual, on the promise of heaven and hell. But autonomy pays a price: by literally taking the place of priests while preaching to their public, narrators and chroniclers act as a secular clergy with regard to their admonitions and bombastic rhetoric.[1]

As a result of the long period of anarchy in Mexican society during its first half-century of independence (1821–63), a time marked by religious wars, church and state were successfully separated. The triumph of the Liberals, and the emergence of a new secular society in a country that had been strongly Catholic, left a huge moral vacuum that needed to be filled. This function was assumed by Liberal writers, the new secular priests, who established themselves as the ethical conscience of society and the builders of a new idea of a liberal nation. Their greatest representative and leader was Ignacio Manuel Altamirano, who articulated his program-manifesto in a series of essays on the national literature. After the Republic was restored, Cuéllar attempted to establish a lyceum for the study and dissemination of literature as well as a newspaper to be called *Liceo mexicano* [Mexican Lyceum]. With that end in mind, on August 4, 1867, in the assembly hall of the San Juan Letrán Theater, he inaugurated a society for the promotion of literature and the dramatic arts, in an attempt to resurrect the famous College of Letrán, which had been founded after Independence by the most important writers and politicians of the first half of the century: Andrés Quintana Roo, Guillermo Prieto, Ignacio Ramírez, Manuel Rodríguez Galván, José María Lacunza, and Manuel Eduardo de Gorostiza. Cuéllar's project, however, failed. In its place he thought of substituting the Literary Salon, whose purpose was to regroup Mexican writers, regardless of their political ideas, under the banner of "Order and Cordiality," a slogan that prefigured the one proclaimed a few years later by the Porfirian regime.[2] Cuéllar, who was on the editorial staff of Altamirano's short-lived *El correo de*

México, played a political role on the paper at a time when many Liberals were fighting against President Juárez. Had Juárez not died in office, a civil war might have broken out. As Altimirano wrote:

> In September of that same year (1867), I founded the politically independent newspaper, *El correo de México*. Joining me as editors were [Ignacio] Ramírez, Guilllermo Prieto, Antonio Garcia, Alfredo Chavero, José Tomás de Cuéllar and Manuel Peredo. This newspaper's objective was to oppose the politics advanced by the government, whose referendum on constitutional powers, which was unpopular and rejected by the entire nation, was a warning. It should be recalled that after 1865 the government of señor Juárez was unconstitutional, and only survived due to the acquiescence of the military leaders, who felt justified by the victory [over the French]. It continued to exist because of the tacit consent of the Republic.[3]

A few years later, with the onset of the new regime, Cuéllar—who never had much influence on the political scene (in this respect, he differed from other members of his generation)—assumed the role of an educator in his *Magic Lantern* series, using his texts much like parables that within a homily serve to censure bad behavior and moralize. For this reason, he declared that if the reader "by the light of my lantern, laughs with me and discovers the folly of vices and bad manners, or is entertained by my models of virtue, I will have won a new convert to morality and justice" (*Prologue*, 4).

What function does the Mexican writer have during the Porifirian Age? It is clear that, as in other parts of Latin America[4] and Europe,[5] once a modern government was in place, the writers who had previously contributed in significant ways to the military and political affairs of their country were displaced and, at times, relegated to minor diplomatic posts (for example, Altamirano, Payno, and Cuéllar himself). Intellectuals would only partially regain their importance in later years during the Ateneo de la Juventud

(1906–13), the 1910 Revolution and during José Vasconcelos's term as Secretary of Public Education (1921–24).[6] Before the advent of the Porfirian dictatorship, literature was supposed to be at the service of the nation, and its function was didactic, as Carlos Monsiváis explains:

> To build the Nation is to create laws, forge a healthy economy, determine positions within society, produce a literature, stipulate the norms of republican morality, and draw on a relevant social psychology. Utopian yearnings are therefore prevalent, whether among politicians or writers who, each of whom in their own way, imagine or dream of a Nation that is also a moral and cultural space.
>
> For the Liberals, freedom of conscience is a prerequisite to progress; if one cannot think freely, one cannot think, and a society that is subject to a single pattern of thought never stops being born. Ignacio Ramírez, Guillermo Prieto and Ignacio Manuel Altamirano *entrust literature with the task of forging a social psychology, and entrust to the chronicle of events and manners the culmination of this project: the reiteration of behavioral characteristics that will be transformed into national traits.*[7]

At the same time Cuéllar was writing for the theater, various authors were portraying Mexicans according to categories, in a tradition that lithography had made fashionable after Independence. The result: a collection entitled *Los mexicanos pintados por sí mismos. Tipos y costumbres nacionales* [Mexicans as Depicted by Themselves: National Types and Customs], published in 1854 by Mungía Press. Its contributors included Hilarión Frías y Soto, Niceto de Zamacois, Juan de Dios Arias, José María Rivera, Pantaleón Tovar, and Ignacio Ramírez. This volume followed the *costumbrista* practice of using words to sketch national types (recognizable through their physiological features). As Sergio González Rodríguez states, this collection presented

> . . . a gamut of portraits that affirmed a taste for the vernacular, for the folkloric, for a realism depicting different villages and

their most picturesque characteristics. Its genealogy had spread since the eighteenth century, when Herder's ideas were disseminated regarding culture as a synthesis of the spirit of a nation. One thus finds an amalgam which arose from the "customs of the century" praised by La Bruyère, La Rochefoucauld and Saint-Simon, or, later, by Voltaire. In the nineteenth century, this literary lineage develops another offshoot in France with Balzac and his "Human Comedy." In Spain, both Larra and Mesonero Romanos would apply themselves to similar endeavors.[8]

Another antecedent to Cuéllar's work is the *Álbum fotográfico* by Hilarión Díaz y Soto, published in 1868 in the famous satiric newspaper *La Orquesta*. Its *costumbrista* approach attempts, through moral portraits, to underscore the main tenets of Liberalism through an anticlerical, nationalist, and republican stance, and by defending the traditional family whose highest value was the decency and virtue of women. It should be recalled that the Liberals placed a great emphasis on the education of females in order to offset the enormous influence the clergy had exerted on women. Cuéllar would continue to support the principles of Liberalism in his novels, in which he harshly criticized the dissolution of the family brought about by the growth of a sumptuous and consumerist economy.

During the Porfirian Age, the role played by literature in forging a national identity slipped into the background; science now came to the fore with a positivist ideology. Significantly, Cuéllar calls his sketches of Mexican characters "physiologies," showing that he unconsciously absorbed the positivist objectives of the "cientificos" (the "Scientists," an elite group of ideologues directing Porfirian society who believed that Mexico would advance through science and technology). Writers born in the 1820s, who were near-contemporaries of Cuéllar (they had fought the same battles and shared the same ideals), dedicated themselves to recreating in fiction the times of anarchy under General Santa Anna. These writers included Guillermo Prieto, in *Memorias de mis tiempos* [Memoirs of My Times], and Manuel Payno, in his novel *Los bandidos de Río Frío* [The Bandits of the Frío River]. Between 1868 and 1875, Cuéllar's chronological contemporaries were producing historical novels set in the colonial period, such as Vicente Riva Palacio's *Monja, casada, virgen y mártir* [Nun, Wife, Virgin and Martyr]; *Las piratas del Golfo* [The Pirates of the Gulf]; and *Martín Garatuza*. More recent historical events were featured in Ignacio Altamirano's *El zarco* [The Blue-Eyed Man] and *Clemencia*. A new concept in historiography was introduced in *México a través de los siglos* [Mexico Across the Centuries], a collaborative work produced by writers and historians including Riva Palacio and Payno. It was as if the profound changes the Porfirian regime had wrought in Mexico made it necessary for the country to revise its most recent history. Cuéllar, however, from 1870 onward, devoted himself to the task of analyzing the great transformations that were taking place in Mexican society during the Porfirian Age, without abandoning the didactic aim that was basic to the Liberal ideology.

Julio Ramos, in his lucid study of fin-de-siècle Latin America, concludes:

> . . . an important project in the intellectual sphere prior to the work of Martí was the rationalization of work, including the subdivision of general knowledge into discourses with differentiated subjects and modes of representation. Modernization was a utopia projected by the degree of formality which writing provided to a world that lacked (although it now desired) scientific knowledge in the modern sense, and which foresaw the dangers of becoming dependent on countries that monopolized that knowledge. In the Republic of Letters, writing gained authority inasmuch as it extended its dominion over the uncertainty and anarchy of the represented world, within a system in which to represent was to impose order on "chaos," "orality," "nature," and "American barbarism." In this way, between literature and the modernizing project (which found a model of rationality and a depository of forms in writing),

there existed a relation of identity, and not simply a "reflection" or similarity.[9]

The Chronicle of the Fin-de-Siècle City

Cuéllar is an urban writer, and his city is Mexico City, where modernity, as in many other Latin American cities, has arrived. The first series of texts included *in The Magic Lantern* were published in 1872, during the era when the Liberal project was consummated. The second edition, which began to appear in 1889, corresponded to an era when peace was consolidated and material improvements to the country were initiated, developments that thereby transformed the concept of urban life. The frequent editions of Cuéllar's novels demonstrate his popularity among the incipient middle class. These novels registered new concerns that set them apart from novels written in earlier periods that had projected a sweeping, epic vision of the country, a vision still present in the impressive work by Manuel Payno mentioned earlier, *Los bandidos de Río Frío* (1889–91). Payno's novel is an immense fresco of the country depicting members of all social classes as they go about their daily rounds. By presenting a wide spectrum of characters, Payno covers every aspect of popular life in Mexico, both in public and in private, while sketching the political, rural, provincial, urban, military, religious, and economic problems of the country during times of anarchy. Cuéllar's texts, published at almost the same time, are intimate, fragmentary, ephemeral, and photographic, and were written for the specific purpose of ridiculing the new customs and manners that replaced the old ones described so well by Guillermo Prieto and Payno. But Cuéllar's nostalgia—the contrast between what was and what is—and his quickly paced chronicles of characters and ways of life that he detests, offer us one of the most polished and valuable portraits of this era, equaled only by Manuel Gutiérrez Nájera, whose chronicles and stories depict the city without the moralizing impulse that tortures Cuéllar.[10]

Vicente Quirarte has reassessed the gaze with which the author of *The Magic Lantern* contemplates his city:

> Even when he boasts about how he has concealed the identity of his characters, Cuéllar speaks not of an abstract city but of Mexico City, with its place-names and landmarks in constant flux because of political necessities and foreign influences. In Cuéllar's novels, a history of the city can be read through its habitats, restaurants, fashions, and places for recreation. It is a city where the national dishes—so succulent, and exalted in detail by Manuel Payno—are replaced by oyster soup, *vol-au-vents*, Westphalian hams, creamed eggs, and chicken marengo, and where pulque makes way for kirchwasser punch, champagne, and Madeira, all part of the arsenal that the procurer Saldaña introduces into the house where the hapless family is having their ball. The restaurants Fulcheri, the Concordia, and the Tivoli of Elysium, which have become small foreign embassies, serve food that tries to whitewash Mexican tastes, just as cold cream cleans the skin of our criollo women, and gloves correct the imperfections of their hands. The exacting standards of the French governess replaces the chaste advice given to young Mexican ladies in the early magazines dedicated exclusively to women. Cuéllar's characters stroll through a city where the prestige of the Avenue of Illustrious Men is the same as the Avenue of Idle Men, which is the name Cuéllar gives the street that is later occupied and ravaged by what Heriberto Frías will call the Pirates of the Boulevard.[11]

Quirarte's description refers to an important literary genre of this fin-de-siècle era, the chronicle, that was employed so frequently by our Latin American writers in the majority of the newly expanding cities. Although Cuéllar's texts are composed as novellas or long short stories, the reader notes a lack of proportion: the descriptions of his characters and their actions are at odds with his moralizing sermons, an imbalance that has led his critics to value fragments of his novels over the novels as a whole. For this reason, individual excerpts taken from the text, purged of the author's zealous moralizing, can be read in part as chronicles, examples of the new genre that replaces an old form of journalism that

> . . . had been the basic means to distribute writing in the period between the emancipation and consolidation of the national states towards the last quarter of the century. . . . [It had been] the model, in its own ordered disposition of meaning, of a rational public life. . . . The chronicle, on the other hand, emerges as a showcase of modern life, produced for a "cultured" reader eager for foreign modernity (Ramos, 92).

Although Cuéllar rejects this modernity in his conscious discourse, the beam of his lantern places it in the spotlight.

The Magic Lantern

What is a magic lantern, and why does Cuéllar collect his work under this title? Right away, it could be said that he is referring to Balzac, since the lantern focuses on society's faults. Our author rapturously exclaims:

> You are absolutely right, Monsieur Honoré de Balzac—you, a privileged man, a profound philosopher, and a connoisseur of society, who with your literary scalpel dissected the human heart, and who, with your superior talents, knew how to enter the spiritual world, and reveal to the world of thought the gloomy and complicated mysteries of the soul; you were right to stop and meditate, silent and absorbed, immersed in the contemplation of that labyrinth of mysteries called the human heart. Lend me some of your sublime admiration, one iota of your genius, a single penetrating gaze, so that I in turn may contemplate my characters, those poor creations that were engendered during nights of meditation and memory.

I, too, long for the improvement of morals; I, too, yearn for human progress and perfectibility; and as a pygmy among writers, I have endeavored to present my types to the world, sending them forth as my feeble contribution to the grand project of universal regeneration.[12]

Though his characters are French, Balzac embraces the whole of humanity in his comedy. Cuéllar limits himself to depicting a local human comedy, uniquely Mexican and nationalist, thereby justifying the aims of his writing. What is most striking is that by using his magnifying lens and appropriating some of the Frenchman's methods in order to focus specifically on Mexicans and their behavior, Cuéllar reveals the dangers to which Mexican families have been exposed by the advances of modernity and the penetration of consumer products from Balzac's country (along with other European nations and the United States), a penetration that would alter the feminine sphere in a fundamental way. Could this, therefore, be considered another foreign invasion, one impossible to contain? The novelist realizes that ever since 1870, the period of the Restored Republic, a new society had been gestating that would later be known as the *porfiriato*, a society in the midst of a definitive transformation, which mobilized as well as dislocated various social, racial, and gender structures and, moreover, displaced those who believed they would triumphantly prepare the way for a new patriarchal society whose spiritual directors would no longer be the clergy but, instead, the Liberals. Cuéllar and other members of his generation were embittered when they discovered that they weren't able to lead this new society, whose control had slipped out of their hands. Through his stories and critiques, however, Cuéllar seeks to return society to the rightful path:

The happy times that have made the Mexican woman a model wife are fast disappearing. The invasion of luxury into the lower classes has muddied the pure wellsprings of domestic virtue, turning modesty and humility into an insatiable desire for fancy baubles to deceive society with a wealth and comfort that do not exist.

Led on by these new yearnings, women have chosen to stand at the brink of a precipice, for they believe they have discovered something superior to virtue in the real world (*Having a Ball*, 80–81).

Mothers and their daughters—mothers of the future—are among the chief targets of the Liberal writers' efforts, much as they were to priests in an earlier era. Fascinated by appearances, by fashion and its dangers, women threaten to destroy the sound foundations of the Mexican society for which the defenders of the fatherland had risked their lives. As announced by Cuéllar in his prologue, the lantern spotlights the characters who make up this new Mexican society:

"What lantern is that?" the typesetter asked me upon receiving the first pages of this work. . . .

"I confess, my esteemed typesetter," I said, "that as to its title, *The Magic Lantern*, I once saw a *pulquería* by that name in a small town; but as to the real purpose of my work, I should tell you that I have walked this earth for many years, searching with my lantern, not like Diogenes, but like a nightwatchman lighting the way, to see what I would find. Within the luminous circle cast by the small lens of my lantern, I have seen a multitude of little figures who have inspired me to draw their portraits with my pen. . . .

"I have copied my characters by the light of my lantern, not engaged in magnificent, fanciful dramas, but in real life, in the midst of the human comedy, surprising them at home, with their families, at work, in the field, in jail, and all over, catching some with a smile on their lips, and others with tears in their eyes. And I have taken special care to make corrections through my profiles of virtue and vice, so that when the reader, by the light of my lantern, laughs with me and discovers the folly of vices and bad manners, or is entertained by my models of virtue, I will have won a new convert to morality and justice.

"This is the magic lantern: it doesn't import customs or labels from abroad; everything is Mexican; everything is ours, important to us alone. We shall leave Russian princesses, *bon vivants*, and kings and queens in Europe, and shall instead be entertained by the Indian, the street bum, the fashionable young lady, the actress, the Liberal soldier, the shop owner, and all that can be found here" (*Having a Ball*, 3–4).

What a curious declaration of principles! Initially, it would seem that Cuéllar is referring to the world of the first half of the nineteenth century, a society that had already been described by Guillermo Prieto in his *Romancero* and then later recreated in *Memorias de mis tiempos*. These memoirs, which Prieto wrote in the 1880s, reveal an unabashed nostalgia for the bustling society that thrived during the years of anarchy, an era that Prieto, as well as Payno, captured so perfectly in their writings. But the "little figures" framed by Cuéllar's magic light are no longer the same: they represent a new national product, the outcome of social changes occurring in the wake of an internal struggle to eject the American or French invaders who are once again present on the national scene, now travestied as agents of order and progress, the price to be paid for modernity.

Christmas Eve

If the modern city grows and is reconstructed during the final decades of the nineteenth century, the spheres of the public and the private are dislocated and reconstructed as well:

The interior—which is fundamental in fin-de-siècle literature—is a space for a new individuality that presupposes a growing dissolution of public and community spaces in the modern city. When he walks outdoors, the private subject—

whose astonishment is implied by his tourist's gaze at the urban scene—seeks to escape the interior, in a gesture which is not necessarily critical, and which demonstrates the need to rebuild and consolidate the fields of collective identity, of class. The city itself (confirming the reterritorializing capacity of modern power) provides the means for the community to reinvent itself. This was one of the functions of the chronicle and the culture industry during the era which marked the passage into modernity (Ramos, 131).

Christmas Eve, the novella by Cuéllar published in Santander, Spain, in 1890 as part of the second edition of *The Magic Lantern*, is composed of short, fast-moving chapters conceived of as photographic "negatives," in the double sense of the word. First, isolated scenes are suddenly captured and frozen as images that, once developed, can be studied with care and made the subject of observation, aesthetics, or memory. Second, if understood literally, "negative" refers to what is deserving of censure, what isn't ethical, the opposite of what one should do. The public and private spheres are turned inside out and reorganized. Cuéllar portrays the interior of a *casa chica* (a "little house," that is, where a married man keeps his mistress), an expression that at once implies the miniaturization of private space and moral degradation. Here, the *casa chica* is the space where the "wife" of a "general" lives, designations that describe a sham, or rather, the rupture of social conventions, or, more simply, the breakdown of the traditional family: a "wife" who is not really a wife, but instead, one of "those women" who is "kept by" "a general" without an army. In other words, these characters have usurped a place and a function that do not belong to them—they are, in short, phonies. The political turmoil the country was subjected to prior to the Porfirian Age caused, says Cuéllar, a vast "*tapestry* of sudden reversals, travels, transformations, and adventures, a fate shared by an incredible number of individuals whose way of life is tied to the agitation and public tumult our country has experienced for so many years" (*Christmas Eve*, 133). During the years of anarchy, these human specimens placed themselves at the interstices of disorder, but with the stability that accompanied the Porfirian Age, they constituted a parasitical element that attached itself to whatever structure would provide security for the time being. These private spaces are not therefore spaces of intimacy, but instead of promiscuity, a promiscuity that arose out of the disintegration of the nuclear family, which was Christian and often rural: "[Pancho] eventually died in abject poverty, leaving several children behind. These did not form a single family, but rather, were scattered and far-flung" (*Christmas Eve*, 134). In several of Cuéllar's texts, the people driven out of the countryside or attracted to the city do not find true accommodations in a city in which structures change and morals are corrupted, where families fascinated by luxury prostitute themselves and turn their women into objects of consumption:

> Once outside *the warp woven* by morality, by maternal love, by an education based on observation and experience, and by a social contract anchored in philosophical ideas, a woman goes forth in the world as part of an immense guild whose members live by their own devices, having broken with the principles of morality, the institution of the family, and the destiny of women (*Christmas Eve*, 134).

It is significant that Cuéllar repeatedly employs a vocabulary associated with feminine tasks (tapestry, warp, woven) to illustrate how a structure dissolves so that it may engender new forms of cohesion. Moreover, the text, in its meanderings, leads us through a variety of spaces: first, the street, a place for meetings, gossip, and quick and lively conversations, an anteroom to the private; and then, within the house, we pass through different interiors: the kitchen, a meeting place for the servants who prepare the special foods that are served on Christmas Eve and during the posadas, festivities that bring together friends and strangers while rumors circulate and abuse, fraud, and promiscuity are given free rein. We then step into the salon, which can be a private space, but which has now been turned into the principal room, for it is here that the ball will take place. We also enter an intermediate space "which had assumed a variety of uses and services" (*Christmas Eve*, 126), a sort of anteroom through which objects and people (the principal and the secondary characters) wander. Finally, we enter the bedroom, the one unquestionably intimate space, where the bed—an essential fixture in the life of a kept woman— is found. Next to the bed is a mirrored armoire in which the "señora" keeps her elegant clothes. She stands in front of this armoire while dressing or, rather, while "correcting" her appearance so that it adheres to the norms of a society in which the woman is the chief sumptuary object.

Judging from her back and arms, this woman was young, delicate, and quite pale. With her fingertips, she pinched the sides of her waist to see if its contours could be reduced by another quarter inch. . . .

These corrections took a long time, and absorbed her to such a degree that not even the noise from the rest of the house distracted her, from which we can gather that her first concern was *to correct* her waistline (*Christmas Eve*, 127).

Artifice takes the place of nature, and the "corrections" alter her appearance so that it will conform to the rules of fashion, to a special Europeanized aesthetic that privileges the white race. Among the skillful operations that allow the city to be reconstructed is also a process of aesthetization that produces a beauty in keeping with this modernization—that is, at the same time the city expands and is reconstructed, women are reconstructed as well, and are adapted to a new concept of urban living.

The stearine candles seemed to aim their rays deliberately at the eyelids of the queen of the ball, and those rays, like doves perched on a marble cornice, cast a shadow onto her eyes which complemented the black line that she had drawn under her lower lid for the first time.

Unbeknownst to Julia, this fortuitous light gave her eyes a value beyond price. The depths of their passion and fire were such that her gaze, which was normally intense and calculating, now had a mysterious, irresistible power. Such is the influence of the lightest touch of the master hand on a line drawn under an eye; such is the effect of a charcoal line and a hint of candlelight on the poor sons of Adam (*Christmas Eve*, 150).

Cuéllar, a partisan of a stratified society in which, from colonial times forward, distinct castes occupied separate niches, here voices his disapproval of the fashion and cosmetics that "correct" the proportions of a woman's body and the color of her skin (her ethnicity), artifices that held Porfirian gentlemen in thrall.

Having a Ball

My gaze rests
on the unstable ship of State,
on public evils, on dangers,
on my beloved fatherland.
It searches our homes
and our manners for that fatal virus which,
as it spreads, corrupts, making
virtue and valor sink, and perverting
the richest and grandest society
until it dies, defiled
by human pride, its towns inundated.[13]

From the epic novel to the *costumbrista* sketch, an enormous distance has been covered by the writer who, before the end of the nineteenth century, is the builder of the nation and the forger of a nationality. Manners have been corrupted and the fatherland— now in lowercase—is sinking, Cuéllar informs us in his despairing poem. What is left for the writer to do? Perhaps, to create texts in which bad habits are ridiculed and defects exaggerated, thereby granting literature a space for reflection, or maybe even salvation:

> In the Republic of Letters, journalism was the site where "rationality," "enlightenment," and "culture" were debated, where "civilization" was distinguished from "barbarism." It is therefore possible to regard the journalism of that age as the site where the polis, the public sector on its way towards rationalism, was formalized.
>
> Also, in another respect, from approximately 1820 to 1880, journalism was the matrix of the new national subject. . . . (Ramos, 92–93.)

Cuéllar, who straddled the two periods, was well practiced in the struggle to forge a nation, and foresaw the obsolescence of his project. He realized he was trapped by the fallacies of the "científicos," who rejected any form of humanism as antiscientific and thus an enemy of the progress and order that had been proclaimed as the dictatorship's motto. Cuéllar's steadfast allegiance to the humanistic seems old-fashioned and romantic:

> I therefore believe that the aim of public education *should not be to spread an enormous mass of encyclopedic knowledge widely and haphazardly*, but rather to devote itself, with profound philosophy, delicate skill, and meticulous care, to an educational system for the people, that has as its moral base the eradication of apathy, wretchedness, uncleanliness, the lack of personal decorum and ambition, the disdain for the comforts of life, low self-worth, and bad manners, laziness, ignorance of public decorum, and selfishness, the lack of respect for women, immorality, drunkenness, and prostitution.[14]

With his lantern, Cuéllar would establish this system of popular education, translated into moralizing maxims, into examples that reprimanded. However, despite his own intentions, as a result of his extraordinarily acute gaze, his ability to reproduce popular language, and his skill at unmasking the private, Cuéllar's work is a perfect example of a discourse that subverts itself by pursuing two contradictory aims: one is deliberate but made superficial by its banal moralizing, while the other (although at times fragmentary) depicts, with a high degree of awareness and reflexivity, the characteristics of the period that he tried to eradicate with his verbal lashings. The first is by choice, while the second is imposed by the weight of reality.

Of all his narratives, *Having a Ball* is the most effective. After first appearing as a serial in a Mexican newspaper, this novel was published in 1886 by Tipografía y Litografía de Filomeno Mata in Mexico City, and later reprinted in 1889 as volume I of the second edition of *The Magic Lantern* published in Barcelona by Espasa y Cía. A provincial family has a ball (that is, a party) where people of all social classes and racial types mix together in complete promiscuity, providing a pretext to gather the whole of Mexican society under the same roof. Payno required more than a thousand pages to contain this society; Cuéllar makes do with a mere fraction: the epic has been degraded. The portrait of manners sketched by Cuéllar is, in his own words, "repugnant," since the concept of "decency" has been lost. An appearance determined by dress eliminates class distinctions, and those who belong to classes thought to have no mobility are able to ascend. "To be" and "to appear" once again define reality; thanks to the artifice of cosmetics and the shamelessness of fashion, a woman appears to be "the other":

> The Machuca sisters kept up appearances, especially the appearance of elegance, which was their ruling passion. They appeared to belong to the Caucasian race, as long as they wore gloves, but when they took them off, the hands of La Malinche appeared on the marble bust of Ninon de Lenclos. As long as they didn't open their mouths, they appeared quite

refined; but their tongues, in the basest of treacheries, betrayed them, making the curious bystander recall the word that served Saldaña so well: "barefoot." And finally, they appeared to be beautiful at night, or in the street, but in the morning or at home, the Machuca sisters were nothing more than dark-skinned girls who had been slightly washed, that's all.
As we were saying, whenever they opened their mouth, the imperfect thread became visible, which was only to be expected, since refined speech, unlike miracle-working satin, is not a piece of merchandise for sale (*Having a Ball*, 29).

A revealing passage, without a doubt. The consumerist society has turned everything on its head. A woman, called a "bauble" by Cuéllar once she loses her "decency" (that is, the decorum of her class and race), becomes merely a item for exchange. Her dress (made of "miracle-working satin") conceals and her makeup creates a facade, yet her tongue exposes her origins: it refers to a social and educational hierarchy. The body can be altered, can suffer metamorphosis, but class, tradition, and good manners are revealed through speech:

Beauty is made, manufactured, arranged through technical means. The body is remade thanks to the corset, the foot is sculpted by the ankle boot; gloves remodel and hats retouch. Honor, traditionally associated with a piece of glass that can be clouded by a pure breath, is exchanged for a mirror that reflects an image of beauty artificially constructed, made complete only if one adopts a ritual of self-scrutiny. The morality yearned for by Cuéllar has been replaced by an aesthetic of appearance and fabrication, by the anti-natural. What's more, artificiality is defined strictly in terms of class: artifice, glitter, and head-to-toe luxury are natural to the upper classes, but the middle-class imitation, in which clothes are put to certain uses, is regarded as dangerous because class boundaries are confused.[15]

Despite his class and race prejudices, Cuéllar is an effective writer in this novel: he was able to map the reciprocal relationships between the elements that constituted the dynamics of a society in the midst of a transformative era—the Porifirian Age, a Mexican-style modernism.

—Margo Glantz
Translated by Margaret Carson

NOTES

1. Carlos Monsiváis, "Las costumbres avanzan entre regaños" [Manners Improve In Between Scoldings], in *Del fistol a la linterna: Homenaje a José Tomás de Cuéllar y Manuel Payno en el centenario de su muerte, 1994*, ed. Margo Glantz (Mexico City: UNAM, 1997), 17. Unless otherwise indicated, all emphasis throughout this preface is mine.

2. See the essay by María del Carmen Ruiz Castañeda, "El Cuéllar de las revistas" [Cuéllar in Magazines] in Glantz, *Del fistol*, 83–97.

3. Cited by Castañeda in Glantz, *Del fistol*, 89–90.

4. "The genre has as one of its zones the function of reformulating judicial relations, of unifying the nation in a judicial manner: this function of the state is carried out in Argentine literature from Independence until the definitive constitution of the State in 1880; the gauchesco genre, more than anything else, covers the integration of the rural masses. The autonomy of literature (its separation from the political and national sphere) is thus an establishment of the political and the State as separate spheres," Josefina Ludmer, "Quien educa" [Those Who Educate] in Filología, vol. 20, 2, footnote 5. Cited by Julio Ramos, "Escritura y oralidad en el Facundo" [Writing and Orality in Facundo], in *Revista Iberoamericana* 143 (April–June 1988): 551–559.

5. Consider the destiny of the French writer Victor Hugo and the feuilletonists (Eugène Sue, Alexandre Dumas) and their failed socialism of consolation. Cf. Umberto Eco, *Socialismo y consolación* (Barcelona: Tusquets, 1970) and Jean Louis Bory, *Eugène Sue, Le roi du roman populaire* (Paris: Hachette, 1962).

6. Cf. Carlos Monsiváis, "Notas sobre la cultura mexicana del siglo XX" [Notes on Twentieth-Century Mexican Culture], in *Historia general de México,* ed. Daniel Cosío Villegas (Mexico City: El Colegio de México, 1981) vol. 4, 3rd ed., 303–476.

7. Monsiváis in Glantz, *Del fistol*, 13. As previously noted, the emphasis is mine, except for the last words in the quote, "national

traits," which the author himself emphasizes. In the same essay, he also adds the following: "Within the political and cultural vanguards the greatest anxiety is caused by the distance that separates the majority of the people from the national idea. Hence the demands for education which, by providing the individual with a general vision of the world, assures him a place in the Nation. For this reason, the worship of history is inculcated, as history teaches personal formation and is the key to understanding and assimilating economic and political processes. . . . By locating the reality of the Nation in the future, it is necessary, without any contradiction, for nationalism (an accumulative passion and sentiment) to become an educational experience. Nationalism: a prerequisite for the Nation" (14).

8. Sergio González Rodríguez, "De lo viejo a lo nuevo" [From the Old to the New], in Glantz, *Del fistol*, 24.

9. Julio Ramos, *Desencuentros de la modernidad en América Latina: Literatura y política en el siglo XIX* [Failed Encounters with Modernity in Latin America: Literature and Politics in the Nineteenth Century] (Mexico City: Fondo de Cultura Ecónomica, 1989), 50.

10. "The city," Julio Ramos also asserts, "an emblem of the desired modernity, was a virtual space for the future" (Ramos, 50). It should be added that there is an obvious difference between the two authors mentioned: Cuéllar is both terrified and fascinated by the transformation of the city he knew into a modern city; Gutiérrez Nájera adores the city with a voluptuous passion.

11. Vicente Quirarte, "Usos ciudadanos de José Tomás de Cuéllar" [Uses of the City in José Tomás de Cuéllar], in Glantz, *Del fistol*, 34.

12. José Tomás de Cuéllar, *Ensalada de pollos* (Mexico City: Editorial Porrúa, 1984), 184.

13. José Tomás de Cuéllar, *Versos, La linterna mágica*, 2nd ed., vol. 15 (Santander, Spain: Blanchard y Cía, 1891), 20. Cited by Antonio Saborit, "Ese deslumbramiento de la linterna mágica" [The Dazzling Light of the Magic Lantern], in Glantz, *Del fistol*, 53.

14. Cuéllar, "La educación del sentido común" [The Education of Common Sense], in *Artículos ligeros sobre asuntos trascendentales*

[Light Articles on Transcendental Matters], *La linterna mágica*, 2nd ed., vol. 21 (Santander, Spain: Imprenta y Litografía de L. Blanchard, 1892), 33.

15. Margo Glantz, *Esguince de cintura* [Cinched Waist] (Mexico City: CNCA, 1994), 27. I repeat here certain ideas from the chapter entitled "De pie sobre la literatura mexicana" [Mexican Literature on Its Feet] from the same book.

THE MAGIC
LANTERN

Prologue

"What lantern is this?" the typesetter asked me upon receiving the first pages of this work. "Who and what will be illuminated by this lantern, and why? Is the title—which would be a good name for a general store—no more than a flashy notice announcing a lot of claptrap, or does the book contain something beneficial for the reader?"

"I confess, my esteemed typesetter," I said, "that as to its title, *The Magic Lantern*, I once saw a *pulquería* by that name in a small town; but as to the real purpose of my work, I should tell you that I have walked this earth for many years, searching with my lantern, not like Diogenes, but like a nightwatchman lighting the way, to see what I would find. Within the luminous circle cast by the small lens of my lantern, I have seen a multitude of little figures who have inspired me to draw their portraits with my pen.

"At first believing I would find something good, I soon realized that this apparatus makes the vices and defects of these little figures more visible; and that, because of an optical effect, these figures become smaller (though some may be as big as an important man), and I can fit them all together, in groups, in families, in public, at meetings, in the army, or in the city. The shimmering rays of the lantern are focused on my characters, and I can see them from within, without resorting to that medical procedure which reveals the interior of the human body.

"Since these characters move incessantly, like ants, I had to become a stenographer and arm myself with a notebook and a pen—though I wouldn't call it a particularly sharp pen, as those are made in London, but rather, one dipped in good-natured ink—and in no time at all, I found myself with a book."

"And this book is the magic lantern?"

"Exactly, young man. But don't fear that I have created terrifying episodes, or will tire the imagination with dreadful tales of horrendous crimes or supernatural acts. I assume, and not without reason, that the public is weary of the thousand and one atrocities that make up many novels (some of them quite good), which go about striking terror into readers and giving nightmares to impressionable young ladies.

"I have copied my characters by the light of my lantern, not engaged in magnificent, fanciful dramas, but in real life, in the midst of the human comedy, surprising them at home, with their families, at work, in the field, in jail, and all over, catching some with a smile on their lips, and others with tears in their eyes. And I have taken special care to make corrections through my profiles of virtue and vice, so that when the reader, by the light of my lantern, laughs with me and discovers the folly of vices and bad manners, or is entertained by my models of virtue, I will have won a new convert to morality and justice.

"This is the magic lantern: it doesn't import customs or labels from abroad; everything is Mexican; everything is ours, important to us alone. We shall leave Russian princesses, *bon vivants*, and kings and queens in Europe, and shall instead be entertained by the Indian, the street bum, the fashionable young lady, the actress, the Liberal soldier, the shop owner, and all that can be found here. But enough for now, my good fellow: I must ask you to end these introductory lines, for prospectuses share the same fate as do several of my acquaintances: they cannot be trusted by their word alone."

FACUNDO

HAVING A BALL

". . . Make sure to invite Camacho . . ."

Preparations for the Ball

I t all begins with a birthday celebration for Matilde, the young lady of the house, and her papa—who loves her dearly, and has just turned a splendid business deal—is going to spare no expense.

More than anything, Matilde wants to dance, despite all the objections of her mama, a respectable, simple woman from the countryside. It is important to please Matilde, and this idea triumphs over all scruples.

"A ball!" her mama said. "How can we have a ball when we hardly know anyone in Mexico City? Who will come?"

"As far as that's concerned, mama, don't worry. I'll invite the Machuca sisters."

"Who are the Machuca sisters?"

"The girls who live across the street. We've started to say hello, and I'm sure that if I invite them properly, they'll come."

"As for me," her papa added, "I'll round up my circle of friends."

"And your lady friends, too?" his wife asked.

"I haven't become acquainted with any yet, but I'm sure many ladies will come."

"Well, as long as you two are in charge of inviting the guests, we can have a ball."

Note that the lady of the house said, "we can have a ball," regarding which a digression is necessary.

To "give a ball" and to "have a ball" are two entirely different matters, as are to "give a dinner" and to "have a dinner."

To "give a ball" means that a person, having chosen some formal pretext, invites his friends to pass a few hours in his company. The pretext is of little consequence. The purpose of the ball is to strengthen the bonds of friendship and forge social ties through an amenable diversion.

In this instance, the friends are the ones who feel flattered and favored; and after attending the ball as guests, they are obliged to call upon the host to express their gratitude, as well as make it known that they wish to reciprocate the invitation to strengthen the friendship.

In the same way, one also gives a dinner, a tea, a concert, etc.

On the other hand, to "have a ball" means to assemble musicians, lights, refreshments, and guests in order to dance, eat, drink . . . and heaven knows what else.

Matilde's mother, as will be seen, wasn't giving a ball— far from it, for what was there to give! Nor was she sure whether it was the same to give a ball as to have a ball, or whether its purpose was to flatter others or to flatter one's self; so that the matter of the guest list—of such importance when one gives a ball—was for Doña Bartola (the name of Matilde's mother) of little concern.

They already counted on the Machuca sisters to attend— those three fashionable young ladies who, judging by their slender waists, their slim figures, and their high spirits, would surely dance up a storm.

And they also counted on a friend of the house who was in charge of "finding couples" to invite a certain woman who had two daughters. It wasn't known what kind of woman she was; but her daughters were, so to speak, of first rank, and this friend guaranteed that they could dance a fearsome waltz. Moreover, because of their strong constitutions, they were unlikely to suffer an apoplexy or fall in their tracks; they had all the traits of *bayadéres*, and could be expected to dance tirelessly.

"Who is the mother of these two girls?" Doña Bartola asked the friend who was collecting dancers.

"She's a bit plump."

"Yes, but . . ."

"As far as 'buts' are concerned, people say she's somewhat merry."

"Merry!" Doña Bartola exclaimed. "Why, so much the better, since it's a dance we're having. What would we do with sad, dreary people! I'd like to meet this merry woman. Invite her, Saldaña, and let the other couples be merry, too."

Saldaña and Matilde's father winked at each other.

"But look here, Saldaña, isn't it true she's . . ." Matilde's father said as he guided Saldaña to his office.

"All her merriment belongs to Don Gabriel, sir."

"Oh! So he's keeping her?"

"Indeed, since last year, and since she no longer flirts with certain young men, evil tongues have been spreading the word. You know how people are!"

"I see. Well, so far we have on our list the Machuca sisters, who are two, I think, and the mother of the two young girls. . . . Will Don Gabriel allow her to come?"

"If Don Gabriel comes, she'll come, too, but nothing can be said to his wife."

"Of course."

"For the same reason, we can't invite Don Pancho or Riquelme because they're friends of Don Gabriel and his wife."

"Yes, yes, Saldaña, that's a good point. I'll leave you in charge of all that; but we need more guests."

"Do you know Camacho?"

"Of course I do!"

"That devil has a gorgeous woman now, and she's quite a dancer! What a waist! What feet! and her—"

"Make sure to invite Camacho."

"I will. What a brilliant acquisition; she's a young beauty he can show off anywhere."

"Bravo! My wife was right: rely on Saldaña, who knows the whole city, and the ballroom will be filled."

"You can rest assured about that. Only don't forget to rent another two dozen chairs."

"They can be rented?"

"Yes, I'll take care of it."

"Thank you, Saldaña, a thousand thanks. You're the man of the hour. And as long as we're on the subject, what shall we have to drink?"

"As for drinks," Saldaña answered, "whatever the budget allows. Champagne and liqueurs, depending on what food will be served. You could offer cold cuts, jellies, and pastries . . ."

"That's good, that seems fine to me: pastries, cold meats, and . . . what else did you say?"

"Jellies."

"Where do they come from?"

"They can be ordered."

"From where?"

"I'll take care of it."

"Splendid, just splendid! Because the truth is, I haven't the faintest idea when it comes to these things."

"You haven't asked the hostess about anything," Doña Bartola shouted. "We don't have any serving dishes, and we're going to need plenty of glasses, plates, and lots of—"

"They can be rented," Saldaña said. "That can all be rented."

"And the silverware?"

"Rented."

"And the tablecloths?"

"That, too. Don't worry about it."

A few days after Saldaña began recruiting guests, a small group of young dandies who had just left the Iturbide billiard hall stopped at the corner of Calle de Vergara before parting company.

"I'll see you tomorrow, Daniel."

"See you then, Gustavo."

"Good-bye, Perico. You'll see—tomorrow I'll beat you," another young man said.

"No, tomorrow I'm not coming."

"Why not?"

"There's a big party."

"Where?" Daniel asked.

"I don't know the street. Gutiérrez is taking me."

"What's this all about?" Gustavo asked.

"Perico's going to a ball, but he's not inviting anyone else."

"Where is it?"

"He says he doesn't know."

"Because he doesn't want us to go."

"Look, why don't you go —"

These young men used words that cannot be printed.

"From the moment he gets up tomorrow, we'll follow him."

"There's no need," Perico proclaimed. "The word's out, so let's all go to the ball."

"Yes indeed, a ball for —"

"Excuse me, but this is a respectable ball. The Machuca sisters are going."

"Now you're going to say we have to wear tails."

A few days after the ball was announced, the Colonel told his wife:

"Bartolita, I think this whole business of the ball is becoming more serious than I expected."

"That's because so many fashionable people are coming. The general's wife asked me what color our dresses would be, and I told her the first thing that came to mind, knowing I would speak with you later. Matilde and I must have new dresses."

"For Matilde, yes—that's already been decided. But as for you—I think the last one I had made would be just fine."

"No, it's too dark. I need a lighter dress and a more stylish one, too. I don't want to be criticized."

"Very well. Tomorrow I'll give you what you need to buy the dresses. The important thing is that they be ready on time."

"Don't worry."

When Matilde received the news, she was happy beyond words.

We have already said that Saldaña was the soul of the party. Without him, no one could have done a thing, not even the head of the household, who was ignorant about such matters, and much less Doña Bartolita who, as she often said, was used to doing things in the ways of her hometown.

Indeed, Saldaña, a most accommodating and useful man, was well informed about everything. He was one of those people who know where you can find good quality at a low price, and can tell you which shoemaker makes patent-leather boots for only three and a half pesos, or where there's a corner tailor who makes as fine a pair of trousers as the master tailor, Salín. He understood all there was to know about rentals and was old friends with Castañares and Barrera, the furniture dealers, and with Zepeda, Gutiérrez, and Noriega, the wine merchants.

"Hello, Saldaña," Don Quintín Gutiérrez said as Saldaña walked into his shop one morning at around eleven o'clock. "What brings you here?"

"Take a guess, Don Quintín."

"Bah! It couldn't be that you've decided our cognac is the best on this plaza."

"Look, you'll never convince me. Zepeda sells cognac that's one hundred times better, and it's cheaper."

"My good man, that's not possible! You don't know what's been said about ours."

"Very well, Don Quintín. I won't stop being your customer because of that. Today I'm here to bring you a little business."

"Whatever you wish, Saldaña. We're at your service."

"Thanks—I see what money can do!"

"Who said anything about money?" Don Quintín turned to his clerk. "Bring this gentleman a glass of the sherry we opened this morning."

"Is it authentic?" Saldaña asked with a doubtful smile.

"I assure you, it's not for sale. I'm keeping it for myself. That is, I wouldn't want even the President to taste it, because I'm sure he'd ask for the entire cask."

The clerk offered the sherry to Saldaña. He pushed his hat back and took the glass with only two fingers. He opened the nostrils of his wide nose as far as possible and inhaled deeply, like someone taking chloroform.

Everyone in the shop was watching Saldaña, and he returned to each a look that spoke eloquently of his approval and surprise. He sniffed the sherry a second time and sampled it without taking a breath. His tongue immediately made a clucking sound against the roof of his mouth. Once more, he sniffed and tasted the sherry, then closed his eyes and exclaimed:

"Don Quintín! Don Quintín!"

"How is it, Saldaña?"

"Don Quintín!"

"Well, all right, let's hear your opinion."

"Don Quintín! Don Quintín!" he repeated, showing his empty glass and stretching out his arm to ask for more.

After getting a nod of approval from Don Quintín, the clerk refilled the glass.

"It's up to you, Don Quintín, but either you sell me two bottles of this sherry or our friendship is over. Whoever heard of such a thing! To let someone taste such nectar, and then declare it's not for sale! As if one came in here just to pass the time. I'll take two bottles, Don Quintín!"

"Are they for you?"

"Yes, for my own personal use. I realize you can't give this ambrosia to everyone."

"It's a deal," Don Quintín said. "You should be proud to be such a fine connoisseur."

"Thank you," Saldaña said, grabbing an oyster-filled *vol-au-vent* and gulping it down in two bites.

"Let's talk about the order, Don Quintín."

The wine merchant opened a ledger and placed an inkwell on the desk. The clerks and the others present turned their attention elsewhere, and Saldaña lowered his voice to speak tête-à-tête with Don Quintín.

"You see, I'm here because . . . Bartolita's husband is having a ball, and I'm in charge of buying the liquor."

"Does he know anything about wine?"

"Forget about it! He doesn't know a thing! You remember the Chateau Lerouse I bought the other day?"

"Of course."

"He thought it was dreadful. He's someone who became rich overnight and thinks that's enough to know all about these waters. That's right, he puts on very elegant airs and likes anything expensive."

"Well then, in that case we'll draw up a special bill . . ."

"And I'll tell you how to make it even bigger, and then we can—"

"Understood."

"... in that case we'll draw up a special bill ..."

Saldaña began to order, asking the price for each item and making a note of it. After making many entries, he decided there would be enough for the guests.

He took another *vol-au-vent* and a slice of ham on bread, then asked for a cognac.

Whenever Saldaña did business with Don Quintín, he always helped himself to a double serving.

How Couples Were Recruited and Guests Invited

There was a mother whose three daughters took the waters at the Pane Baths* almost every day because they needed it. These three girls had three admirers who took the same waters, but without needing it. Since this mother had younger children as well, she stayed at home, and the three girls rode the public coaches that make the rounds of the watering places.

On entering the coach, they would find one admirer already seated there, and a few stops later, the other two would hop on board.

Through this hydrotherapeutic regime, the girls' health improved bit by bit. They came home wearing a towel down their back to receive their damp, curly manes, which were held in place by a narrow blue ribbon that went around the nape of their neck and was tied in a bow where their hair parted. They smelled like naiads and emanated the essence of algae; and the freshness of

---

* One of several spas in Mexico City popular among the middle class.

their skin announced the voluptuousness of their personal care. Their tiny hands were pale because the cold water sent the blood away from their fingers to where it was needed most. Their cheeks, however, had the rosy blush of a ripening apricot. A drop or two of water, still caught in the tendrils of their hair despite the rumble of the carriage, quivered like pearls of dew between the stamen and pistil of a musk rose.

The girls were fresh and clean, and they experienced the voluptuous tingling caused by the cold-water reaction, which allows the body to feel the caress of its own blood. Their epidermis had been cleansed of secretions, and their pores felt as though kissed by oxygenated air.

They felt the comfort of an anonymous caress which they could savor with their heads raised, without embarrassment. Even the touch of their clean underclothes was somewhat tender.

This physiological state added a little more sparkle to their eyes, and an added radiance to their smiles.

In short, the girls not only looked fresh, but they felt good.

That was precisely what their mother and Dr. Liceaga* sought. By enhancing the body's circulation, hydrotherapy bestows on the nervous system—which is so delicate, so exquisite, and so obedient—a far from negligible amount of what can be called "the joy of living," creating an atmosphere in which half a dozen love-stricken youths feel as though they are on the true road to happiness.

After this bath (whose temperature quickened their physiological reaction), these nymphs and their tritons in round hats continued to bathe each other with looks, with light, with atmosphere, and with hopes.

The girls hoped to dance, that is, to climb the stairs to happiness in one bound, bringing the cold-water reaction to its fruition on an elegant carpet and, while tête-à-tête with a young man, enjoy intimacies granted a stamp of approval by society.

The young men had tracked the scent of a ball to Doña Bartolita's house, and they searched for a means to gain entry along with their girlfriends.

---

* Eduardo Liceaga (1839–1920), a physician and advocate of hydrotherapy who was president of the Mexican National Academy of Medicine.

During their carriage-ride, they plotted a scheme in short order. As it so often happens with these young dandies, they understood each other almost without words, no doubt because, physiologically speaking, there is very little that separates a coldwater bath from dancing the habanera. And so on that very same day at about two o'clock, one of these admirers (the most daring) called on the mother of the three girls, accompanied by a young cavalry officer who was a complete stranger to the house.

Their mother (who, as we have said, was a good woman) came out to greet the callers, and was introduced to the captain. A short while later the three girls appeared one by one, each with a plush towel down her back and a curly, fluffy, thick head of hair.

The captain smelled a nymph-like fragrance that gave him goose bumps.

"This gentleman," the young man said to the girls' mother, "has come to invite you to a ball."

"Well, thank you," their mother said without hesitation.

"It's going to be a fine ball," the captain added. "The Machuca sisters are going to be there."

"Oh! That means it will be a fancy affair," she replied.

"Not exactly," the captain answered. "But I guarantee you, it's a very respectable home."

"I've heard it's going to be a very good ball, too," one of the girls added.

"May I tell the Colonel you'll be there?" the captain asked the mother.

"What colonel?" she asked.

"What do you mean! The colonel of my regiment, the one who's giving the ball."

"Oh! So you mean he's your colonel?"

"Yes, ma'am, and Doña Bartolita, his wife, sends word that even though she hasn't had the pleasure of your acquaintance, she would be most honored by your presence."

"You see, mama?" one of her daughters said. "The señora herself is inviting us. Isn't she kind! We mustn't disappoint her."

"Naturally," the captain said. "I can tell that your mother is an elegant woman, and isn't capable of such a slight."

"Of course not," the young man said.

The mother, who was tongue-tied in front of the captain, feared she might commit a social gaffe by turning down an invitation from such high quarters. She nodded her consent.

The captain and the young admirer departed, and the three girls finished drying their hair.

All the while, Saldaña never stopped to rest. He was a man who took his business to heart: he was eager to be of service as an emissary, and, moreover, he was dying to do business with people of a certain importance. He entered the National Palace and asked to see the director of one of its offices, but was shown to the waiting room just like anyone else. However, he convinced the doorman that he was no mere supplicant, but a close friend of the director and, most important, that he had come there on family business, on an entirely personal matter. The doorman led Saldaña to another door and spoke to its keeper. Moments later Saldaña was in front of the illustrious personage.

"What is it?" the illustrious personage said, ushering Saldaña to the side because he knew his visitor's business was best discussed in private.

"Nothing, only don't make any plans for Saturday."

"What do you have in mind? That stubborn blonde again . . ."

"No! It's got nothing to do with a blonde! I'm going to take you to a little ball."

"Look, my friend, with those kind of women . . ."

"It won't be like that. It's a ball at the home of Colonel ——" and Saldaña gave his name.

"I don't know him. Who's going?"

"I'm counting on the whole gang. Miguelito and Don Cruz and Acevedo are going."

"Oh! Well then . . ."

"But don't get the wrong idea. Respectable young ladies are going, that's all."

"Do we know them?"

"Of the ones we know, the Machucas."

"Oh!"

"And the three girls who take the waters at the Pane Baths."

"What are their names?"

"Isaura, Rebeca, and Natalia."

"Oh, yes! And is Don Gabriel's lady friend going?"

"Yes, and Camacho's, too."

"Really?"

"He just told me so."

"Well, then, I'm going, too. Where's the house?"

Saldaña wrote down the address on a scrap of paper, gave it to the director, and strutted proudly out the door.

Matilde's papa had arrived home earlier, and he waited for Saldaña to report on his thousand errands.

"Where have you been?" Doña Bartolita asked her husband.

"I went to Lohse's to buy some candelabras."

"More candelabras?"

"Yes, my dear, can't you see we don't have enough? Remember, we're talking about a ball, and at a ball . . . well, just imagine, at a ball . . ."

"Yes, yes, and did you buy them?"

"I did, and each one holds six candles."

"And where are they?"

"They'll be delivered this afternoon."

"Good. And what about inviting the guests?"

"I've done all I can. Would you believe, the clerk at Lohse's is a young man . . ."

Matilde, who at that moment was doing needlework, raised her head.

"A young man with blond hair," her papa continued, "so friendly, so refined, so . . . I mean, he's a gentleman, and since he showed me so many candelabras and went to such trouble, I thought it was only natural to invite him."

"Well done. We'll show everyone that we're not snobs. After all, balls were made for young men. He must have been thrilled."

"Oh! As happy as could be. He says he likes to dance and . . . he's a decent boy and says he knows you and Matilde . . ."

"Who is he, dearie?"

"I don't know, mama. I think his name is Carlos; he's the one who sold us the silverware and the trays."

"Can you imagine, I didn't even notice him?"

"I didn't either," pretended Matilde. "But I think it must be him."

Once this method of inviting guests was put into practice, it wasn't long before the whole of Mexico City was coming to the ball. Saldaña invited his friends, who in turn invited their mistresses, making it logical to conclude that everyone's mistress would be there, and that the ball would be the merriest in the world. Doña Bartola was right: a merry crowd is essential at a ball. The woman about whom Doña Bartola made that remark had, according to Saldaña, nothing to be merry about besides the fact that Don Gabriel was keeping her. But her presence was advantageous for two reasons: first, because she dressed so well, and second, because she had two daughters.

This woman had not always given rise to gossip, nor had she always dressed so elegantly. It all depended, as her husband explained, on the circumstances.

Consider, if you will, that this same husband had gotten himself into a fine mess, and all because he took so much pity on a client that he set her up in her own house, and as the house was a great expense, his budget was thrown entirely out of kilter. There began his troubles. That year the business in his district was

"... she became another person."

hardly profitable, and the poor notary began to feel he was between a sword and a wall. And then, with so many temptations
and so many devils to be tempted by, he signed an agreement.
Oh, ill-fated signature! Would you believe that was the start of
everything? But he had no choice: the notary tarnished his im-
maculate honor by signing his name, and he entered into (as he
admitted) a shady operation. However, though his conscience
tweaked him, this business brought him some very good times,
indeed, so good that his wife began to feel jealousy stirring inside
her like a demon. But even that turned out well, for he began to
court her once again, buying her presents and asking her to dress
elegantly and wear makeup. It was he who introduced her to face
cream and powder and provided her first lesson. How beautiful
she looked! You have no idea how much she improved with that
face powder; she became another person. She wasn't bad looking

at all, but because her complexion was somewhat dark, you could hardly notice her lovely eyelashes and fine eyebrows, or appreciate her full garnet lips that, when set off by the bismuth-white powder, became . . . I can't say how provocative. Imagine, even the notary himself, who had been married to her for so many years, found something new in his wife. And just to show you how men are, on the day the bismuth powder was inaugurated, Don Gabriel—a lifelong friend of the lady's family, no less, who had seen her countless times without finding anything subversive about her face—couldn't take his eyes off her, and he felt . . . love, that's right, love, emerging from that calcareous powder like Venus from the foam of the sea. Don Gabriel was surprised at himself, and he mulled over the fact that in all the years he'd known her, he had never noticed her charms and . . . and . . . would you believe . . . what a coincidence! While Don Gabriel was excavating his love under the geological layers of her face, the notary—that is, Don Gabriel's lifelong friend—found himself at the brink of a precipice. His shady business collapsed, and the poor notary, who had tasted the pleasures of the good life as well as those of infidelity, was now about to crown his glories with nothing less than a jail term. Now you see why I mentioned coincidences: the only one who could save him from going over the brink was Don Gabriel himself.

Now imagine, if you will, the esteem the notary accorded Don Gabriel; the esteem Don Gabriel accorded the notary in return; and most important, the esteem they both accorded the notary's wife.

As the results show, these three people esteemed each other so highly that the lady, who we could say had entered her second youth, had never been so happy; she was much happier than when she had a dark complexion.

Ever since her skin took on its Germanic whiteness, this lady moved by different springs, and as she was prompted by other motives (such that she no longer arrived at Mass with her usual punctuality), she became very conceited, especially with respect to her shoes. Don Gabriel himself, among the countless favors he rendered, often carried in his bag a pair of colorfully embroidered satin shoes lined with silk, so small they made him laugh.

This lady likes to walk up and down Calle de Dios and Calle de Ayuntamiento showing her precious little feet, which are exquisitely displayed in shoes (because Don Gabriel doesn't like ankle boots).

As the curious reader must have realized by now, Don Gabriel was rich, that is, he grew rich during the halcyon years we have just passed through.

Don Gabriel was only scraping by before he made contact with the public sector; but once initiated, he went from being a poor man to what is called "the newly rich." In no time at all, Don Gabriel could count his income in the thousands. Pesos rained on him from all directions: truly, it was a blessing from heaven. And there you have him, spending his pesos like an English lord! What a house Don Gabriel had! Never had such a house been seen before in Mexico City. What a staircase! What patios! The hallways, the curtains! Oh! The curtains, the upholstery, the pillows, all were made from gilt-trimmed satin. Indeed, people vied for an invitation to visit this wonder.

Now tell me if Don Gabriel, as rich as he was, couldn't do something to save the poor notary from the catastrophe that was threatening. A word from the lady sufficed, and the matter of Don Gabriel's signature and the rest of the paperwork was arranged as if everything had been swept clean. Afterwards, the notary radiated contentment, his wife glowed with youth (her second), and Don Gabriel gleamed with gold and satisfaction.

Even though everyone knew the notary's wife was being kept by Don Gabriel, appearances were maintained. The notary paraded his wife on Sundays, and she looked beautiful, simply ravishing, in a brightly colored dress festooned with ornaments and trim. She stood in perfect contrast to the good notary, a creature of habit who didn't mind going out in a corduroy suit and an old pair of boots. His drab wardrobe paled in comparison to his wife's splendid attire, especially under the glare of the same midday sun.

On the occasion of the ball, Saldaña thought that the lady would prefer to go with Don Gabriel, and he believed, as we have seen, that he was being very diplomatic and proper by not inviting her husband; but it so happened that in the frenzy of inviting everyone, a third person had invited the notary. Because the invitation had been issued twice, and from different sources, the happy threesome—that is, the notary, his wife, and Don Gabriel—felt even more obliged to attend. For the lady, it was an opportune turn of events (as was everything that had happened to her recently) because with all the talk of the ball and how fine it would be, Don Gabriel, showing his customary generosity, offered to take care of her daughters' toilette, and the girls felt almost as happy as their mother.

As for Isaura, Rebeca, and Natalia, the preparations of these fashionable young ladies had a distinctly different character, because when you're poor, appearances count for everything. Isaura cut up a lime-green dress, bought several yards of jade-green silk and another few yards of emerald ribbon at the Portal de las Flores, and then stitched up a green dress that was more than she could have asked for.

Rebeca, however, did ask for more, and a close friend provided the means to rescue her from her plight. As for Natalia, her mother turned a frayed skirt into a jacket that, according to her sisters, was just the thing.

Their mother already knew that she would go in her usual black dress because, as she explained, old ladies aren't favored by flashy colors or trinkets. Indeed, she had a point—she didn't wear them well at all. With that and with having lost her looks as a result of misfortunes, illness, and hunger, she stood in perfect contrast to her daughters, who were always the first to imitate the latest extreme in fashion.

III

About the Machuca Sisters and Others Like Them

Word spread all over town about Doña Bartolita's ball, as some called it, or the Colonel's ball, as others said; but to the invited guests it was known as Saldaña's ball since, as our readers are well aware, he was the one in charge of invitations, among other things.

He couldn't pass up the opportunity to swell the ranks of the invited: he entered the Concordia Restaurant and found a general of his acquaintance eating breakfast.

"Good morning, General!"

"How are you, Saldaña, how goes it?"

"As you can see, General, I'm earning a living," Saldaña answered, taking a seat across from him in a familiar way.

"Anything new?"

"What do you suppose, General! A ball! And listen—it's the kind you don't see much of these days."

"How's that?"

"Well, I'm making the arrangements."

"You?"

"Yes, General, I'm in charge of the wine and the invitations."

"Ah! So you're inviting the guests . . ."

"Yes, and I'd like to extend a formal invitation to you, General. Come to ——," and Saldaña told him where the house was.

"And it's going to be quite good, eh?"

"Oh, yes—the Machuca sisters are going."

"They are?"

"They'll be the first to arrive."

"And who else?"

"Oh, some real beauties—Don Gabriel's mistress and Camacho's, too."

"That slender one?"

"Yes, the one with the tiny little waist and the tiny feet and the . . . well, in a word, Camacho's mistress. How could I have failed to invite Camacho?"

"You mean, this ball will have—"

"There will be some very fine girls there, General. Don't miss it."

"Who's giving it?"

"Ah yes, I forgot to tell you. He's the colonel of——" and Saldaña named an army regiment. "Be sure to come, General. There will be some excellent wines; I just placed an order with Don Quintín Gutiérrez. Remember: it's on ——, number—— this Saturday night. As I said, the Machuca sisters are going."

We don't know why, but the general thought what many other people thought when they accepted Saldaña's invitation: this ball would be a good one because the Machuca sisters were going.

The general hadn't yet paid for his chocolate when a friend came over to talk.

"Good morning, General, how are you?"

"How goes it, Peña?"

"Not bad. You're looking at a very satisfied man."

"Did you win the lottery?"

"No, General. But I've just been invited to a ball."

"Which ball is that?"

"A very good one—the Machuca sisters are going."

"So the Machucas are going?" the general asked almost mechanically.

"The Machuca sisters are going, yes sir, the Machuca sisters will be there."

"Hey, Perico," a young man just entering the Concordia said to his friend. "Don't miss the ball on Saturday. The Machuca sisters are going."

"Who would miss it! Even if he's limping!"

The general and Peña gave each other a knowing look.

"Everyone is talking about this ball," Peña said. "And the most remarkable thing is, they all say it's going to be good because the Machuca sisters will be there."

"And who, once and for all, are the famous Machuca sisters?"

"What! You don't know them, General? Then you haven't been to the Zócalo,* the music hall, the circus or anywhere!"

"I'm not saying I don't know them. I know them perfectly well—who doesn't? What I mean is I don't know who they are."

"Ah, General, as far as that goes. . . . First of all, let me tell you that they wear beautiful clothes. Yes, indeed! How beautifully they dress!"

"I've already noticed that; but . . ."

"About their finery: I assure you that—"

"Yes, but tell me— where does it come from?"

"I'm getting there, General. It's a question of provisions."

"Come on, Peña, that's very mysterious."

"There's no mystery. Everyone knows about it."

"But who supports them?

"They depend on . . . you'll see. Gumesinda, the shortest one, the one whose eyes are . . ."

"Yes, I know her."

"Well, that one . . . she's not really a Machuca. She's an Obando, or more precisely, a Pérez de Villar, because Obando had already separated from his wife when—"

"Just a minute! Don't go so far off the subject. Let's just agree, like everyone else, that those two are Machucas. Now tell me, without beating around the bush, who supports them, who maintains them, who . . ."

---

* The central plaza in Mexico City, also known as the Plaza de la Constitución.

"Their upkeep is no problem because their brother, Machuca the paymaster, is a despicable coward, as you know."

"I know his story: when the Plan of Tuxtepec* was proclaimed, he came into his own because he knows people in high places."

"And ever since then," Peña added, "up, up and away! You know, this is the age of cowards. So he lined his pockets, General, or as he says, he put something away for a rainy day."

"And he's the one who . . . ?"

"Let me continue . . . the truth is, Machuca's real sister—not Gumesinda, the other one, Leonor— well, when her daughter was born . . ."

"Ah! So she had a—"

"Yes, General, that's why they left town, and ever since then, their brother no longer pays the dressmaker's bills."

"Ah!"

"Now you understand his prestige among the people upstairs."

"Yes, I already knew that."

"Now, as for Gumesinda—"

"Not only Gumesinda, but the other one too, the youngest, because there are three Machuca sisters."

"She's not a Machuca either. If you take a good look at her, she seems more like Leonor's half-sister. I don't know her last name, but frankly, I have my suspicions."

"Well, that's enough." The general said good-bye to Peña and left the Concordia, resolving not to miss the Colonel's ball so that (among other things) he could look closely at the Machuca sisters.

Although the fame of the Machuca sisters was universal, the same was not true for their brother. He was known in his office, at the Treasury and in some other places, but he wasn't very fond of public appearances. In fact, in order to give himself more room to operate, he gave his sisters free rein; and they, quite naturally, did whatever they pleased, which suited them perfectly.

The Machuca sisters had been very poor, miserably poor, indeed so poor that whenever Saldaña, who knows everyone in

* A reference to the proclamation dated January 1, 1876, in which Porfirio Díaz was named commander of the insurrectionist army attempting to overthrow President Sebastián Lerdo de Tejada. In May 1877, Díaz became President of Mexico.

Mexico City, is asked about their background, he says that he knew them when they were "barefoot."

Indeed, the Machucas could never have imagined that they would arrive at the pinnacle at which they find themselves today, thanks to their scheming, conniving brother who, as his sisters say, is capable of squeezing money from a stone (which isn't as far-fetched as it sounds, since some believe he has a share in the contract to supply the paving stones for Calle de Plateros). The Machuca sisters kept up appearances, especially the appearance of elegance, which was their ruling passion. They appeared to belong to the Caucasian race, as long as they wore gloves, but when they took them off, the hands of La Malinche* appeared on the marble bust of Ninon de Lenclos.† As long as they didn't open their mouths, they appeared quite refined; but their tongue, in the basest of treacheries, betrayed them, making the curious bystander recall the word that served Saldaña so well: "barefoot." And finally, they appeared to be beautiful at night, or in the street, but in the morning or at home, the Machuca sisters were nothing more than dark-skinned girls who had been slightly washed, that's all.

As we were saying, whenever they opened their mouths, the imperfect thread became visible, which was only to be expected, since refined speech, unlike miracle-working satin, is not a piece of merchandise for sale.

Let us observe them with one of their trusted friends, with whom (as they said) they had nothing to hide because they had all grown up together.

This friend walked through their bedrooms until he found them, as if he were a king in his own castle. "What are you doing, Gumesinda?"

"You can see for yourself, old boy, I'm combing my hair."

"Did you take a bath?"

---

* Reference to Doña Marina, the indigenous woman who was Hernán Cortés's mistress and translator.

† Lenclos (1620–1705), famed for her wit and beauty, hosted a French salon frequented by prominent literary figures of her day (La Fontaine, Racine, Moliére).

"Damn! What a lot of questions you have!"

"Don't get angry. Are you in a bad mood?"

"I'm fit to be tied."

On the whole, the Machuca sisters had very bad tempers. All three indiscriminately used the interjection "old boy" no matter whom they were talking to. "Damn," an expression they learned since they met Saldaña, was another characteristic trait of their oratorical style.

One of the reasons the Machuca sisters were so celebrated and well known was that their brother, who prided himself on being a dyed-in-the-wool Liberal, had unintentionally established in his home the right to assemble and freedom of conscience.

The Machuca sisters and their visitors took it upon themselves to establish their remaining rights.

Once this democratic system was in place, not a week went by when they weren't having fun at a picnic, ball, or outing. They were as ready to go on a trip to the countryside as they were to attend a wedding, and never stopped to find out who the host was, or the name of the bride and groom.

Many men visited them, but few married women. The sisters themselves admitted that in order to socialize with these ladies, they would have to be very careful and very courteous, which was something they weren't used to.

On this point Machuca agreed with his sisters.

One of their visitors was an unassuming gentleman somewhat along in years who had light gray hair, a moustache, and blue eyes. He was, by all accounts, a rich man who knew how to do business, although he wasn't a lawyer. He made a living by bartering trinkets, acting as a middleman, and making deals, and he was quite successful.

He had a certain something that is almost impossible to say in Spanish, because it doesn't give an exact idea of what this gentleman had. Latin is required: he had, as it were, *coram vobis*,* which

---

* *Black's Law Dictionary:* "Before you. A writ of error directed by a court of review to the court which tried the cause, to correct an error in fact." Most likely, Cuéllar wishes to suggest that this character was successful because he had good connections.

is one of the most useful things to have in Mexico City in order to get ahead.

He looked like a seraphim, or as the saying goes, as if he couldn't kill a fly. He hardly ever laughed, and his movements were slow and deliberate, but there were still some traces in his physiognomy of what had made him a fine young man twenty years ago.

What this preamble leads up to is that this gentleman was one of the most love-besotted men ever known. In all senses of the word, he was a lover by profession: he came into the world with an essentially erotic mission, and was soon overcome by philogyny, a condition as incurable as an organic lesion.

This man had a wife and daughters, but it was as if they didn't exist. As a result of his joyful adventures and infidelities, he had been separated from his wife for years. However, having yielded to his irresistible matrimonial tendencies, he had another family to provide for, and they cost him a fortune. Yet this was no obstacle to his supporting three additional households, each of which allowed him to savor in small doses, and in shifts, the delights of fatherhood.

He was so enamored of that trifle called woman that, despite all his present satisfactions, he took whatever woman was offered to him, just to avoid saying no. Yet this man, who everyone said had a "roving eye," did not rove in the least! On the contrary, he was austere and reserved; but that didn't prevent him from carrying out his mission with the tenacity and industry of a watchmaker.

He kept a standing army of ladies who belonged to him, yet still had time to have the occasional dish à la carte at the inn.

This man would often visit the Machuca sisters, and his presence in their household would alarm the other visitors, as a cock disturbs the chickens in a henhouse.

We don't want to give him a name for fear he might resemble someone, and then we would be blamed for drawing portraits instead of presenting types, thereby breaking the laws governing the novel. However, since it is necessary to distinguish him from our other characters, we will use a name that has nothing in common with the persons he may bring to mind: we will simply call him Don Manuel.

When Don Manuel entered the Machuca house, some of the visitors lowered their voices, others left, and others made faces. But his arrival always made the course of the conversation change, to the extent that the girls said "damn" on fewer occasions or hardly ever.

Another thing the Machuca sisters were fond of was gambling. You see how peculiar they were! But they lived to beat the odds, and they played with an admirable innocence and naïveté. At the fair in Tacubaya* and elsewhere, they entered the gambling den with the same aplomb and ease as they entered the circus, for it never crossed their minds that games of chance are degrading. Because these girls had been poor and, moreover, had different mothers, with each mother having a more or less complicated and shameful history, they had grown up as best they could, as weeds grow despite the cobblestones above them: they grew because of the weather, the atmosphere, and the laws of Nature.

They had never owned anything back then; but they always had something to eat, and always had clothes, mostly shabby, to cover themselves; that is, they could be seen in public, or rather, their nakedness couldn't be seen. The fact is, they had somehow reached adolescence, and had no desire to look back. Today they enter the world on easy street, and are guided by the occasion, with no scruples or fear. They are happy, but with the blind happiness of those who never stop to consider why things are the way they are.

These sisters had silk dresses and jewelry, but never thought that such a wardrobe came at the price of their brother's honor. They were pleased to be sought after, never realizing that they attracted vultures looking for corrupted flesh. They played games of chance in order to feel the gamut of emotions between winning and losing, without considering how shameful these recreations are; nor did they consider that at those green baize tables they put themselves on the same level as the prostitutes and the cardsharps

---

* Tacubaya, a former indigenous village to the west of Mexico City, became in the mid-nineteenth century a fashionable resort town known for its ornate Italianate villas, gambling houses, and fairs. Tacubaya is now a district surrounded by the greater metropolitan area of Mexico City.

at their sides, those social outcasts banished by morality from the fellowship of honorable people.

The Machuca sisters lost their brother's money and their own reputation in Tacubaya, then went home beaming with happiness. They were so free from worries that no one could have made them feel ashamed of their behavior. Those poor Machucas! Today there are many young women just like them, lured into the gambling den by a flood of immorality that has led to the debasement of all our manners!

I V

In Which, Among Other Things, the Girls Who Frequent the Pane Baths Prepare Themselves for the Colonel's Ball

Isaura's green dress was ready, and Natalia's skirt had been transformed into a jacket, but the girls still lacked certain indispensable devices that are designed to do nothing short of correcting, or rather, distorting and exaggerating, the proportions given them by Mother Nature.

With the sharp eye of the young lady of fashion, these girls had noticed that today's woman should display a protruding curve in the region of the coccyx, neither more nor less than the size of an abscess, an unusual fibroid, or the hump of a dromedary, and there's no point in asking them why. Fashion has dictates that proper girls obey like galley slaves.

Paris has taken charge of correcting her figure, of enlarging, whittling, and streamlining it in order to distance her more and more from our first mother in Paradise. If the shoulders of Eve and her daughters could be called sculptural because of their

". . . and tried to fit her with a little basket."

roundness, these days that lady's descendants prefer that their
shoulders be pointed and angular, in order to prove that the curve
is not the true line of beauty. They wear shoes whose toe is like
the tip of a pencil, and they pile other protuberances onto their
shoulders that remind one of the claws on a bat's wing.

As we mentioned earlier, these girls were poor, and they had
already spent what their mother's budget allowed, exhausting
their monthly allowance (as an army garrison does) in just
twenty-five days. It was impossible for them to buy one of those
cages made of stays and ribbons that round out a woman from
behind. But Isaura was a resourceful girl, and wouldn't let such a
minor detail keep her from improvising such a cage.

She took her sister Rebeca aside and tried to fit her with a little
basket. Natalia favored a breadbasket, and made very sensible
claims for its flexibility and light weight. And their mama, who

couldn't help but applaud their ingenuity, came into the room carrying her own makeshift solutions.

"No, mama!" Natalia exclaimed, annoyed. "How could we wear a bird cage or a cigar box!"

"It's to fill you out!" their mama said. "No one will notice."

"But you can feel it! And it's hard . . ."

"And the shape—it should be soft and flexible, as if it were made from whalebone," Rebeca said.

"You mean, a real bustle," their mama answered.

"Yes, like the ones they sell in *La Sorpresa y Primavera Unidas* for twenty reales." Rebeca said this while wearing the basket in the place under consideration.

"Someone's at the door!"

"Ave Maria!"

"Keep the door closed! We're not at home!"

"Who could it be?"

"Whoever it is, don't open it!"

"I can't get the basket out! It's caught!" Rebeca exclaimed.

"Hide the cage!"

"Those baskets, too!"

"They've gone away!"

"No, they're still knocking!"

"It must be a friend!"

"Don't pay any attention!"

"It's open!"

"Oh, dear Jesus!"

Pío Cenizo, one of their admirers, had just entered. He had barely greeted them before he noticed that something extraordinary was happening. Isaura turned pale, Rebeca was struck dumb, Natalia began to tremble, and their mama quivered.

"What happened?" Pío exclaimed. "Some disaster?"

No one could answer. Pío looked all over.

"Did the bird get out?" he asked, noticing the cage.

"Yes, my canary," Natalia said, discovering her refuge.

"What a shame!" Pío said. "Did it sing?"

"Yes, beautifully."

"And how did that rascal escape?" he said, examining the cage.

"We just realized—four wires are missing. A buzzard could have fit through. No wonder he escaped!"

The girls burst out laughing. Rebeca had to walk backwards to leave the room because she hadn't freed herself from the basket yet.

"Why so many baskets?" Pío asked. "I suppose you want to catch the runaway."

"That's it," their mama said. "We were going to set a trap."

"Set a trap? That's what I'm here for," Pío said. "I'll catch him. Do you think he's on the roof?"

"That's where he's singing, you can hear him there," their mama said.

"Then that's where I'm going!"

And Pío Cenizo headed for the roof.

Preparations were quite different in the home of the notary's wife. Her two daughters had been given magnificent satin dresses made by a first-rate dressmaker. Don Gabriel's lavish gifts dazzled the notary and his wife. Not only were they dazzled, but they were also left speechless; and when the notary's wife saw Don Gabriel, she could barely pronounce these words:

"Why have you taken such an interest in their . . . dresses?"

The notary, who couldn't utter a word, reminded himself that the greatest eloquence is found in silence.

Saldaña, who for many days thought of nothing else besides the ball, took it more to heart than anyone else, not only because he treated everything that way, but because, more than ever before, he wanted to delight in the pleasures of a ball, and especially this ball, since it was practically his. He had done everything; it was his creation, his work, and he intended to enjoy himself to make up for all the trouble he had gone to. The idea of dancing and wearing his finest inspired him to look in a mirror. His everyday suit was too short, it wasn't dark enough, and it was threadbare. How could he attend the ball looking like that!

But for Saldaña it wasn't a problem, because once he had made arrangements for the liquor, rentals and all the rest, a little something was left over that he called, in complete conscience, a "commission," resting his claim on Article V of the Constitution,[*]

---

[*] Refers to the Mexican Constitution of 1857.

which prohibits any work or personal service that is not justly compensated.

Armed with his constitutional rights, he went straight away to a corner tailor who was also a friend, in fact a very good friend, and who was nothing less than the Saldaña of tailors because he made the most of all varieties of secondhand clothes: from the tails of a frock coat he created a vest; and from a suit with worn elbows he created a new suit for a boy. In other words, he specialized in transformations.

"Hello, Don Teodoro, how are you?"

"Hello, Saldaña, what's new?"

"Nothing, just a ball."

"I've already heard about it—they say it's the Machucas' ball."

"What do you mean, the Machucas' ball! They'd better call it Saldaña's ball, because I'm the one who's planning it."

"Of course. And it's going to be good, they say."

"So good that I need your help, Don Teodoro."

"Let me see what I can do . . ."

"I need a frock coat."

"Black?"

"Of course, it's for a ball!"

"Here's one lined in silk—a magnificent garment and a real bargain. It belonged to a congressman . . ."

"Ah! I know the story. Let me tell it to you, Don Teodoro. This is the new frock coat that a congressman wore six months ago to a banquet in the Tivoli de San Cosme where, as you know, because of a question over some floozy, he got into a scuffle. He wasn't hurt, but his frock coat came out of it with a big rip and a consommé stain. When he arrived home, still tipsy, he handed the coat to his servant and declared, 'Take this away! I never want to see it again!'"

"That's right, and the servant sold it to me," Don Teodoro said. "Look at it now; try to find the rip or the consommé stain."

"It's brand new!" Saldaña exclaimed. "And you must have given the servant a few pesos for it."

"That's right! I gave him five so that I could sell it for fifteen."

"Fifteen pesos for that disgusting rag!"

"It's brand new."

"I'll give you eight."

"That's good money, but it's worth fifteen."

After a great deal of discussion, Saldaña settled on the frock coat for nine pesos.

He immediately went to his shoemaker, the one who made patent leather boots for three and a half pesos. He also bought a tie, and used benzene to soften a pair of gloves he'd had for six years, since he only wore them on formal occasions (of which he had known few).

"It's splendid!" Saldaña proclaimed as he tried on the frock coat. "I look like a king. I'll create a sensation! The only thing that's missing is a good chain for my pocket watch. . . . You'll find a way, Saldaña." He tapped his forehead a few times. "I just remembered! My poor Lupe! The mother of my children! With all the excitement over the ball, she hasn't received her daily allowance for three days! I've left her without any money! Nothing! She must have pawned some things by now, poor thing. . . . I'll drop by to see her on my rounds."

Lupe was neither his wife nor his mistress in active duty; according to his classification, she belonged to the Archives: she was the mother of his little ones. Likewise, in his absence Lupe called Saldaña "the father of my little ones." With that having been said, it should be clear that this temporary union had no moral ties besides those little ones.

But at the thought of having left his Lupe without any money, Saldaña was seized by a nostalgic love, and felt a vehement desire to have her take part in the pleasures of the ball, where he intended to be completely happy.

"Good morning, Lupe," he said as he entered. "Where are my little devils? Look sharp! Come here, my boys."

And a little boy climbed up on each knee.

Lupe was stirring a pot of rice. She turned her head to Saldaña.

"Have you been sick?"

"No, my dear, I've been busy, terribly busy. What about you?"

"My aches have returned."

"You haven't found a cure?"

"No."

"Look, woman, what you need is a little excitement."

"What do you mean?"

"Let me tell you. Have you heard about the ball?"

"Last night in the courtyard the neighbors were talking about a ball, and since your name came up, I paid attention."

"Aha! So you know that I'm the one who's arranging everything—it's my ball. I mean, I'm not paying for it, not that, but I'm putting it together and it's going to be splendid."

"That's what they say."

"And I've got it stuck in my head . . ."

"What?"

"To take you with me."

"Are you crazy?"

"No, I'm longing to dance with you like . . . you know, like we danced before . . ."

"Yes; but that was back then," Lupe sighed.

"And now? Yes, sir, why not now? Look, to make sure we understand each other, I'm eating here today," he said, lowering the boys from his knees. "What do you have?" he asked, approaching the fire.

"Nothing but rice."

"Well, today's a holiday. I'll treat," he said, stroking her pale cheek with his bony hand before going outside.

All the while Lupe hadn't stopped stirring the rice. When she recovered from her surprise and added water to the pot, it began to burn. Steam billowed from the pot and spread the essence of onion throughout the room, awakening the appetites of the children, who asked for soup in unison.

A few minutes later Saldaña reappeared, followed by a boy carrying some covered dishes, bread, tortillas, and a pail filled with pulque.

"Lupe, look!" Saldaña exclaimed as he uncovered the dishes. "Turkey with mole sauce, enchiladas, tortillas and beans, and pulque to go with it all."

The little ones toddled over to the delivery boy and stood on tiptoe to smell everything. A wave of gastronomical delight passed through Lupe's system, which contrasted with the shadows of her usual sadness.

Saldaña managed to place a small wooden table on the uneven planks of the floor. There were only two chairs to go with the table, so the children sat on a trunk.

During lunch, and between glasses of San Bartolo pulque, Saldaña explained to Lupe that he would bring her a dress, a fan, and everything else the poor woman would need to play, at least for a night, the part of a well-to-do lady. This wasn't the first time Saldaña had entertained such fantasies. Lupe listened with resignation, but outwardly seemed quite willing to be transformed.

The next day, Saldaña entered a pawnshop managed by a Spaniard, a friend of his, whom he called over to the end of the counter.

"Look here, Don Sotero, we can redeem the blue dress," he said, taking out a large wallet bulging with all kinds of paper. "Here's the ticket. My clients will pay up to fourteen pesos if they like it."

"No, my friend, the owner said at least sixteen pesos."

"I think he'll come down by two pesos."

"Don't be so sure, Saldaña; that's the lowest he'll go."

"Well, all right, I'll take it and see if my clients will pay the two extra pesos."

A clerk sorted through a few familiar bundles and handed one over to Saldaña.

Meanwhile, Saldaña took out another claim ticket and said:

"I'll give you five for the fan."

"Six is the lowest."

"All right. I'll take that, too, and I'll see if I can get the other peso. So in total, twenty-two pesos. I thought it would come out to nineteen, but there you are. I'll be back, Don Sotero."

"Good-bye, Saldaña."

Several more steps had to be taken to furnish Lupe with an outfit. When at last he believed nothing more was needed, he headed back to the home of his little ones.

The dress had to be taken in at the waist and shortened a bit, but Saldaña was quite sure that Don Sotero wouldn't notice. He would, of course, return the blue dress and the fan on the day after the ball, with the excuse that his clients wouldn't pay the three-peso difference.

It was resolved, then, that Lupe would go to the ball. Saldaña was surprised by the thought of her transformation. He was terribly pleased by all he had done, and he told himself:

"Magnificent! That's called having compassion. Why shouldn't I invite that poor woman! She more than deserves it for all her years of resignation and selflessness. Lupe, the poor thing, never has any fun. She's only gone to the puppet show twice, and that was when she took the boys. Just think, I took away all the comforts of her life and because of me she lost her boyfriend and . . . in short, I made her the mother of my little ones! It's important for her to dance and have a good time. We'll leave a neighbor in charge of the boys. I'll ask a close friend of mine to be her escort, and the ball will more than make it up to him for his trouble. Once she enters the room, who the devil will guess that Lupe is . . . the mother of my little ones!"

Preparations for the ball were under way all over town. The fact is, these preparations were neither more nor less than they were for any other ball, and if it weren't for the order established by this present account, they would have gone unnoticed. But a novelist has, among other rights, the right to enter his characters' homes whenever he pleases, with the pious intent of publishing their secrets.

So let us once more drop in on the Machuca sisters, for we shouldn't pass up the opportunity to analyze the particulars surrounding them. The Machucas, among their many bad traits, danced the habanera very well, indeed so well that on the eve of the ball, they had each promised more habaneras than could possibly be danced in a single night. We maintain that to dance the habanera well is a bad trait, and if the curious reader is patient, he'll hear directly from us why.

In the never-ending battle that morality wages against vice in every society, hypocrisy prepares the transactions through which evil habits are spread.

Hypocrisy is a kind of business agent for vice. It lets a religious holiday take the blame for offenses against morality, and combines the Feast of Candlemas with the open operation of gambling dens and the proliferation of scoundrels.

Meanwhile, "those ladies" and married women play the odds together while staking their looks, their husbands' money, and their children's bread. This transaction is allowed to take place with no more conditions than that it be temporary and somewhat removed from the center of town. Propriety has reconciled itself to the professional spitter or the emphysematic, as long as he doesn't spit in the center of the room, but in the corner and into a spittoon.

Since the fair is located in Tacubaya and lasts a few short weeks, the shame and immorality of the gambling den is, for some ladies, no more than a pardonable lapse.

Let's look at another transaction. Hypocrisy believes it is proper to say farewell to the pleasures of the flesh before the terrible prospect of forty days' abstinence, and invents Carnival. Back when the prostitutes in Mexico City were "barefoot" (like the Machuca sisters when Saldaña first met them), the masked balls were, without exception, for the upper classes. However, ever since luxury and prostitution have shaken hands, these balls have been populated by "those ladies," and the male sex takes advantage of this annual event to indulge in pleasure without any qualms or inhibitions.

At last, we reach the transaction we started with: the habanera.

The poor slaves in Cuba, baked by the sun, scarred by the whip, and brutalized by their wretchedness, will one day wake up to the rhythm of music, just as a snake sleeping under a rock wakes up.

In the life of a savage or a slave, pleasure is essentially for reproductive purposes, for the same physiological reason that an animal feels pleasure for a certain period in its life. For the slave and the animal, then, pleasure doesn't exist without lust, and since dancing expresses pleasure, the dance of the slave couldn't be anything but libidinous.

The slave has every right to dance this way under the blazing sun, just as a lion in the desert has the right to roar in pursuit of a lioness.

At the same time that these roars and dances appeared, the minuet and the quadrille were losing favor in tropical lands, and hypocrisy found the occasion to introduce a dance innovation.

Young girls were as blindfolded; they didn't understand a thing about roaring lions or Negro dances. In fact, they thought it was a harmless novelty to keep time with their hands and feet, and they danced the habanera right in front of their papas.

And all the papas gave this Negro dance their seal of approval for the ballroom, even before hypocrisy could intervene.

And another irrevocable deal was struck between morality and evil habits.

Having made the foregoing observations, and in light of our earlier comments, there is no better way to make the nature of certain characters known than to repeat what everyone says: the Machuca sisters dance the habanera very well.

V

Concerning What Happened to the Virtue of a Lady Invited to Saldaña's Ball

Around this time, a family moved into new quarters, and, to judge from all appearances, they had suffered a sudden reversal in fortune.

The older woman was short and dark-skinned with long, bony hands, and her manners were far from refined. Accompanying her was a very elegant young lady and a boy about twelve years old. No one would have believed that the older woman was the elegant lady's mother. So many differences existed between them that it hardly seemed possible that this daughter could have descended from such common stock. The mother was unkempt and the daughter was well groomed; the mother, vulgar and common, the daughter, elegant and well educated. If we were to look into the moral consequences of these differences, we would discover that neither mother nor daughter had much affection for the other.

This divine young lady was often applauded by her male admirers for making such impudent remarks as:

"There's nothing worse than a mother!"

They were constantly quarreling with each other, and the daughter would often exclaim, "Oh, mama!" in tones ranging from contemptuous to irate. By every measure—their character, education, physique—mother and daughter were exact opposites.

The mother, who in her day had lovely eyes and a somewhat provocative national "charm," had crossed paths with one of those carefree Don Juans for whom each stage of life is marked by a new love adventure. A short stay in the town of Orizaba,* and a picnic interrupted by a cloudburst, brought Enriqueta into the world, and ever since then, her mother has turned her disgrace into a *modus vivendi*.

The truth is, once Enriqueta was born, her mother didn't have a thing to worry about. Enriqueta's father dearly loved his daughter, and he was, moreover, a wealthy man who needed to keep up appearances and avoid scandal.

That is how the curious reader can account for the substantially different complexions of the mother, Enriqueta, and the twelve-year-old boy, who was toasted as dark as his mama.

These girls with rich papas and poor mamas are, on their maternal side, from the lowest rungs of society, and have entered the world through a breach opened by a rich man's escapade. They float between the two currents until they drown in mud.

On the whole, the devil luxury is responsible for this disastrous plunge.

Enriqueta was now nineteen years old. She had gone to good schools and made aristocratic friends. True, she hadn't learned much (as fine as these schools were), but she had learned to dress well. Nothing vexed her more than not having a new dress to wear or not being able to buy the most expensive boots in the store. Her mother accompanied her everywhere, always walking a few steps behind. Enriqueta was slender, had straight posture, and moved gracefully. She always wore the most unique hats she could find in the fashionable stores. Her mother, on the other hand, wore a black veil and a black shawl and, on holidays, a woolen coat with hardly any trimmings.

* A resort town in the mountains east of Mexico City.

As long as his circumstances allowed, Enriqueta's papa provided for everything this splinter from his family needed. Then, when he least expected it, things started going downhill, and Enriqueta and her mother passed through some of their darkest days, which seemed even worse because nothing had ever been denied the girl before.

Fortunately, as her mother said, Enriqueta's suitcase was well packed, and she could weather this bad stretch for some time.

And that, in effect, is what happened. Not many weeks went by before Enriqueta (after a long conversation with her mother about what course of action they should take) began to sit at the window. She was sad, and it was plain to see. Of course she was, if her boots were worn down at the heels and her mama wasn't able to buy a new pair. The outcome of their conversation was this: Enriqueta didn't know how to do a thing, and, besides, she wasn't born for work; and as to her mother, although she could sew (her one and only skill), she wouldn't earn enough to pay for their food. The terrible truth revealed itself in all its naked deformity.

Enriqueta's mother realized that her daughter would do anything besides work to provide for herself; and Enriqueta, filled with all these thoughts, found no other way to console herself than by sitting at the window.

This window, the only one in their small, run-down apartment, looked out onto Avenida Juaréz, which was always so busy, especially in the afternoon.

A few days after Enriqueta first sat at the window to get some . . . air (since air is so necessary for life), she already had four admirers. It was difficult to choose among them, especially since any boyfriend of hers would have to possess many qualities.

One afternoon, before Enriqueta dressed herself to sit at the window, there was a knock at the door. A large woman dressed in black with a shawl over her head was standing outside.

Enriqueta's mother opened the door.

"Good afternoon, señora, how are you?"

"Come in," the mother said to be polite.

"Thank you, thank you," the visitor said as she entered. "What do you think about this heat, my dear? My word! I'm suffocating! I've come from so far away! Do you smoke? Have one of these, they're Aztecas wrapped in corn-husks for ladies. There's nothing better, above all for your chest, and with this cough of mine. . . . What can I say? Old women like us are good for nothing."

Meanwhile Enriqueta's mother took one of the Aztecas and rolled it in her fingers. The visitor took out some matches and offered her a light.

"Light up, my dear. The two of us can . . ."

"Thank you."

"Not at all. Aren't these cigarettes smooth? What kind do you smoke?"

"These are the ones I usually smoke, but at the moment . . ."

"Take this pack. I've got two, and besides, I'm always on the street and can buy them easily. Take it."

"But . . ."

"It's a poor gift, I know, but please do me the favor of accepting it."

"Well, thank you very much."

"Now, the reason I came," the old woman continued, "is to let you know that this apartment shouldn't have been rented. I mean, it's not your fault, my dear, and may God forgive me but . . . believe me, the rent on this apartment has already been paid for six months."

"What! For this apartment?"

"Yes, this same one."

"But I just finished paying the rent in advance."

"That's the scam. These landlords are sharks, and they'll do anything for money. My dear, don't let them take you for a fool. If you only knew what was going on. . . . Of course, you know the person who paid the rent."

"No, I don't . . ."

"What! You don't know Manuelito?"

"Manuelito . . ."

"Yes, Manuelito, that's what I've called him all these years. I've known him since before his whiskers started to sprout. . . . But yes, Manuelito, Don Manuel as he's called, is a good boy, my dear, and I've never seen anyone as honest as him. Yes, he's someone you can have dealings with. He's the complete gentleman. And what's more, he's loaded with pesos—Manuelito's rich from head to toe, and it's not the kind of wealth that's only for show. And what a table he sets! What I mean is, he lives like a prince."

"Oh, yes! I know more or less who you're talking about. Yes, how could I not know who he is?"

"Isn't that the truth, my dear? It's what I've been saying! It's impossible not to know Manuelito."

"So he's the one who . . ."

"The one who paid the rent for six months, and you should know, my dear, the reasons why. Let me tell you some things about Manuelito. There was a family living here—well, not exactly a family. There was Maria, her little sister, an aunt, and a maid. And just to let you know how foolish people are—can you believe that this girl Maria, who was so well dressed and who . . . because there was nothing she lacked—what lovely dresses, everything was beautiful! You see, she was Manuelito's, and so of course she was fitted out like a queen, and I tell you, he didn't visit her more than two times a week. What more could the little fool have asked for! But it was all for nothing! The devil gets inside of women. And this Maria, as beautiful as she was and all, ran off one night before sunrise. Who do you think with? A lieutenant, a boy that's worth nothing, and there you have her poor aunt who had to return to Puebla all because of this silly girl! But what else can you expect, my dear? We women are ruled by evil. I never would have done that! If I were the target of Manuelito's favors, I would hold onto him for the rest of my life."

Enriqueta's mother didn't have a chance to take a breath or utter a sound before the old woman continued:

"Yes, my dear, so I said to myself, I'm going to see about that apartment because someone could be making money off it, and if there's one thing that cries out to heaven, it's that this apartment has been paid for six months and maybe some poor person is making a sacrifice for the rent. So you see, my dear, in times like these, it's worth it to . . . since no one has money to throw around, well then, if it seems like a good idea to you . . ."

"But what's the best thing to do?"

"Well, that's for you to decide, my dear. As for me, I've done what I could by telling you. When all is said and done, maybe someone will be helped, and I believe in doing what's right, no matter who benefits. That's why I set out from my house on Estanco de Hombres, by tram, of course, because it's too far to walk."

"But I couldn't think of it," Enriqueta's mother said, "I know Don Manuel by sight, but . . ."

"I understand, my dear, I understand; and you're absolutely right, especially because when a favor is granted, it must be granted all the way. Don't you agree? And I . . . well, why deny it? I get what I want from Manuelito. Imagine, he was still a baby-faced kid when . . . and ever since, he keeps me in mind, and . . . oh, if it weren't for him! . . . upon my soul! My family would have gone hungry so many times! Think of it: a widow with no man in the house, and burdened with sons. But there was food, thanks to God and Manuelito, yes, there was food, and how can I be ungrateful? I've got two of my boys, the oldest ones, in jobs, and the youngest has his tuition paid by Manuelito as if he were the father. So . . . you just need to make up your mind, and if you want to . . ."

"But I don't know how."

"It's very simple, my dear, very simple; I simply need to mention the rent to Manuelito and tell him that you are . . . well, I don't know, maybe you're rich, but even still, it wouldn't hurt to have something extra."

"Rich! How could I be rich, señora?"

• "My name is Jesusita, María de Jesús, but everyone calls me Chucha. You were saying, my dear? I don't know your name, either."

"Dolores."

"Well then, Lolita, you were saying that . . ."

"I'm not rich, and quite frankly, that six months' rent would suit me just fine, especially for my daughter, the child of my peccadilloes."

"What! You have a daughter?"

"Yes, señora, Jesusita or Chucha, as you prefer, I have a daughter."

"Really!" the old woman said, pretending she didn't already know. "And how old is she? She must be in school."

"School! She's a grown woman!"

"Oh! But I didn't know!"

"Enriqueta!" her mother shouted. "She must be at the window. It's her only entertainment."

"The poor thing! Leave her alone, it's not right to—"

"Enriqueta!" her mother shouted even louder.

Enriqueta soon appeared.

Chucha stood up and exclaimed, "Blessed Virgin! What a lovely creature! So this is your daughter? Ah! Lolita, your daughter is . . . simply exquisite!"

"You were calling me, mama?"

"I called you so you could meet—"

Her mother didn't dare say Chucha or Jesusita because her woman's intuition told her more or less whom she was dealing with. And what's more, she was certain that this business of the rent was no more than a pretext; but to nip her remorse in the bud, she conjured up the image of her own poverty, and recalled her deep meditations over the past few days while she searched for some way to escape the crisis in which she found herself.

After coldly greeting this stranger, Enriqueta returned to her place at the window.

"Well, then, Lolita, it's all very simple. If I tell Manuelito to see you, everything will be fixed. He's such an honest man . . . do you think he'd let the landlord feed from two troughs? Manuelito doesn't have to pay in this case, but even if it meant paying thousands of pesos, it wouldn't matter. . . . Lolita, my dear, no praise is high enough for Manuelito. Well, I'd better be off. I have to take the tram and transfer to the Central Line, and then see after my boys. What else can I do? When you're all alone. . . . Lolita, it's a pleasure to have met such a fine person. María de Jesús Pinillos, at your humble service, Estanco de Hombres number———, first door on the left. Good-bye, my dear! No long farewells; I don't want you to stand in this draft and catch one of those bad colds that are going around. Good-bye!"

And the old woman disappeared without taking a breath, leaving an ecstatic Doña Lolita behind.

It was about six o'clock in the evening.

The sky began to assume that flaming, sinister-like color that gives wise men so much to ponder. The cosmic dust, they say, steals its radiance from a crepuscular zone far above the atmosphere that wraps the Western hemisphere in a reddish vault, making the sky resemble the roof of an oven faintly lit by the agonizing flames of the last piece of wood.

This color fell directly upon Enriqueta as she sat by the window. Her lilac-tinted dress was like an amethyst, and her face took on a rosy glow. When she raised her head, as though drawn into the luminous red zone spreading above, her eyes had a peculiar glitter.

Shadows had already descended upon Avenida Juárez. The sidewalk and buildings formed a large black mass from which strings of yellow lights sparkled like gold sequins on a black velvet mantle; these were the gas lamps that were hidden by the trees lining the Paseo de la Reforma. Small red lights, flickering like the embers of burning paper, traveled two by two in an endless procession; those were the lanterns of carriages returning from their outings. These restless, wavering, small lights could have been mistaken for the fiery eyes of a pack of monstrous wolves searching for the dark.

Enriqueta was quiet, but sat up straight, with a red flower on her chest. The celestial colors still highlighted her lilac dress against the dark background of the window.

The heavy, monotonous rumble of the carriage wheels on the uneven paving stones sounded, at times, like hailstones, and at other times, like a waterfall whose muted echo becomes louder or softer depending upon the gusts of wind.

Enriqueta not only felt the impact of these reverberations on the malleus and anvil of her middle ear, but from time to time she felt vibrations tingling through the soles of her boots. These sensations were like a surge of current from an electromagnetic machine, and they exerted a certain voluptuous influence on Enriqueta.

Enriqueta sat there as if on display to the world, stationed like a beggar in a doorway asking for alms. But what Enriqueta sought was not a daily pittance: she wanted luxurious alms from an opulent society. She fixed her eyes on the train of carriages carrying the rich. Her pupils darted restlessly as she gazed into the interior of a landau and looked at the driver's seat and the Frisian horses. She examined the silhouettes of four young men in a phaeton, and looked at footmen in livery standing beside black, red, and chestnut horses wearing lustrous harnesses. She surveyed the family carriages, buggies, victorias and coupés; studied the profiles of ladies and the backs of gentlemen; and peered into open doors, discovering cushioned interiors, hat plumes, gloved hands, and beautiful women lost in shadows. Everything was in motion, creating fleeting images that barely left an impression on her retina before being erased by another image, and then another, in a never-ending vertigo.

Enriqueta's senses were wrapped in a grand, worldly caress. She was stunned by the rumble of the carriages, much as a big kiss can take one by surprise. The dizzying stream of fugitive images made her eyes light up in amazement at this great spectacle. The trembling pavement sent a kind of magnetic tickling from her feet to her waist, and a moist breeze saturated with the smells of dirt, carriage wax, and English leather harmonized all her sensations. And just so as not to exclude her sense of taste from this sensual *quorum*, her dainty teeth chewed on a rose petal, which made her mouth water.

Young ladies who sit at the window in order to be seen have an invisible little genie behind them advising them to tighten their corset and arrange their hair: this is Love.

Yet behind Enriqueta there was no smiling, playful, shy Cupid, but a cruel, tyrannical, despotic witch carrying a gold scepter, who subjugates half the world and laughs at poverty.

Her name is "fashion," and she is created by luxury. That naïve and spontaneous Cupid in the Age of the Patriarchs is now a mere go-between for all the Enriquetas at their balconies who are searching for wealth.

Enriqueta, like many elegant young women, couldn't conceive of naked love; it was too mythological. She couldn't imagine love without opulence, which explains why she looked into the depths of a carriage or into the facets of a three-carat diamond.

While Enriqueta sat at her window, entirely given over to the rapture we have attempted to sketch, Doña Dolores, the mother of this elegant young lady, stayed in the room where Chucha had left her, immersed in deep thought.

There was no light left on the horizon other than the blazing celestial phenomenon whose rays still outlined Enriqueta's lilac silhouette against the window. Meanwhile, the room where Doña Dolores sat was completely engulfed in shadows.

Enriqueta's mama understood everything. She accepted this stroke of good fortune with her eyes closed; the darkness of the room suited the occasion. In order to cast out the remorse that stabbed at her, she reasoned that Enriqueta's lot couldn't have been any different: such was her destiny. In their current straits it was crazy to think that Enriqueta could find a rich boyfriend. They were saved; a door opened out of the limbo of their misery; there was no other escape. Nevertheless—and we say this to commend Doña Dolores—she couldn't stop two fat tears from rolling down her cheeks and falling onto her hands, which she held tightly clasped to her bosom. As her tears fell, she trembled with terror and shame.

By now, the twilight colors had completely disappeared. It was pitch-dark, and Enriqueta withdrew from her window.

As could be expected, Don Manuel appeared at their house the following day. He asked for Doña Dolores, who received him with some trepidation, as his presence fulfilled the dark thoughts that had tormented her the previous afternoon.

Don Manuel sat down and said nothing. The prologue to a new love story is always awkward, even though Don Manuel, a man of the world, well knew how these matters, after following different paths, all converged on the same point. Experience had shown him what luxury, interest rates, and necessity tended to do to a girl's virtue, yet he couldn't disguise his natural reluctance to bring up this matter with a mother.

Enriqueta's mother didn't dare break the silence, either; as a victim, she thought it sufficed to lower her head.

Under these circumstances any pretext or incident, even a sigh, was needed to start the conversation. Don Manuel was searching around the room for some such excuse, when Doña Dolores took out her handkerchief to daub at her eyes.

Don Manuel found the start of a paragraph in the handkerchief.

"Please, señora," he exclaimed, "there's no cause for distress."

This sentence produced the opposite effect: Doña Dolores burst into tears.

"Don't worry, señora. Please calm down; everything in life has a solution. I can't bear to see tears or misfortunes, and my greatest desire is to be of service to those in need. As far as the rent on this house is concerned, rest assured that the next six months have been paid. Now then, if there are any other matters that trouble you, and if I inspire your trust, by all means tell me what you need."

Doña Dolores dried her tears. Realizing that the step over the precipice was easier than she had imagined, she answered:

"Any other troubles! Do you think it's amusing to be a poor woman like myself, without any support, abandoned long ago by the father of our love child . . . yes, that's what I should say, abandoned, because I've written him four letters with no reply, so I shouldn't expect anything from that end."

Don Manuel had found the opening, and began to question her. Doña Dolores dropped her reserves before this liberator, and described her life from even before that cloudburst at Orizaba, the one that interrupted an afternoon picnic and served as Enriqueta's introduction to the world.

The poor woman knew perfectly well where her confidences would lead, but she wasn't brave enough to turn back. She quickened her step in order to arrive sooner at the precipice that, through an ironic twist of fate, she had chosen as her salvation.

Enriqueta didn't take part in this conversation until later, when Don Manuel was about to leave, and she hardly exchanged any words with him. The opposite, however, would be the case in the future.

It is during these six months that we have reason to speak of Enriqueta, for she was one of the young girls invited to Saldaña's ball. Since Don Manuel, a businesslike man, was Enriqueta's protector for designated hours only, she had free time to dispose of, and she indeed disposed of it, generally in the company of a friendly and entertaining young gallant. At his request, Enriqueta asked Don Manuel for permission to attend Saldaña's ball, which (as should be obvious by now) had created a sensation in half the city.

Saldaña's fine eye for choosing the right girls for the ball, his numerous personal contacts in every social circle, and the ample funds given to him by the Colonel, have given us the opportunity to introduce our good readers in advance to the cast of characters at that ball, one of many in Mexico City that have come to justify the old saying, "A crowd is not company."

On the list of people to be invited (a list Saldaña always carried in his pocket), a certain name appeared: "Venturita . . ."

It was the only name that trailed off with dots. Who was Venturita? She was a young woman . . . but not so young in the true sense of the word. She was one of those women who seem to reverse course and attempt to undo the steps that time has forced them to take.

Venturita had a difficult role to play in the world: she was a sister-in-law. She had neither father nor mother, and her home was the home of her married sister, on whose husband she, of course, depended.

Venturita carried within her soul the memory of a heartbreak, the source of all her sadness, romanticism, and even coquetry. This heartbreak gave shape, color, and character to everything she did. If it were possible to read a person's deepest thoughts and secrets in an instant, we would, at times, declare someone completely mad who had never before showed any sign of being obsessed by a single, solitary idea. Well then, Venturita was such a case.

Ever since the aforementioned heartbreak, there wasn't a thing about her that wasn't somehow linked, including her gestures. When she raised her hand to her forehead: it was the heartbreak. When she woke up late: the heartbreak. When she ate very little: once more, the heartbreak.

She went out to walk the streets or sat on a bench in the Alameda Park; she attended Mass and kneeled for an extra quarter of an hour; she sighed for no reason or became very talkative: it was the heartbreak. It was all inescapably due to that heartbreak, which would be part of her for the rest of her life.

What else? Her elegant, pretentious wardrobe, the color of her dress fabric, and even the extra little tug she gave to the lacing of her corset, all had the same source: the heartbreak.

Let's take a closer look at the nature of this heartbreak. Venturita was the older of two sisters. What's more, there were two brothers who came between them. Not only was Venturita the oldest, but she was also the prettiest, and everyone thought

Venturita would certainly be the first to get married. But just the opposite occurred: her brothers and sister married and Venturita stayed single, yes, single, right up to the present, and now the poor thing was going through some very bitter times indeed. Venturita thought her bad luck with men would never end, because when it comes to questions of love, she has been one of the most unfortunate women ever known. It wasn't that Venturita was ugly, no sir, as you yourself can judge by the following.

She was somewhat pale, but not because of illness or weak blood; she was pale because the colors of youth that had graced her cheeks for more than the usual time had departed, as they always do, and neither she nor anyone else could be blamed for that.

Venturita still had beautiful eyes. They weren't dark enough, nor were her lashes thick enough, to be considered typically Mexican;

but they were sparkling and expressive, especially when she decided to fight against her bad luck with all her might.

What was beyond reproach was her body. Her shoulders and shoulder blades had more than enough time to reach their full development, and the constant use of a corset had forced her ribs to give way to the whalebone's tyrannical pressure. Those well-developed shoulders and the pressure from the stays had traced lines onto her body that were forcibly oblique and pleasingly curved. They culminated in an almost unbelievable waist that produced a certain tingling in the palms of any man who desired to measure its subversive circumference with his hands.

This matter of the curves and the tingling hands was revealed to Venturita by a close friend, who had heard about the tickling phenomenon directly from her lover. He in turn had learned about it in strictest confidence from some of his friends.

Ever since then, whenever Venturita sat at her dressing table and adjusted her corset, the order of thoughts passing through her mind was: first, the heartbreak, and another tug on the laces; and second, that tingling sensation in the palms of the opposite sex. All considered, it could not be denied that Venturita had a charming waist, which might explain why she was always warm; she hardly ever wore a coat, even in the winter.

Whatever belonged to Venturita had its own unique stamp. A shoemaker on Calle del Reloj who had made her shoes for many years was well aware of his customer's aesthetics, for she returned more pairs of shoes than she kept.

Venturita's artistic knowledge and her special study of the shoe made her an intelligent connoisseur of the effects and consequences of its contours.

Venturita always dressed well and wore fine shoes. She walked wherever she could be seen, or wherever the most people were, because she was certain (and justifiably so) that she was eminently presentable. And when she displayed herself on Sundays and holidays between noon and one o'clock in the Zócalo or on Calle de Plateros, it was not with the same intentions and designs that certain women have, no sir: Venturita's were perfectly legitimate. She wanted to get married, she wanted a suitor, and there is nothing reprehensible in such an aspiration. What else do pretty girls want? We have even more reason to excuse Venturita's stratagems, for she needed them a hundred times more than most young ladies do—first of all, because the days go by, and Venturita grows older and older; and furthermore, the thought of being a perpetual sister-in-law was unbearable, particularly when it concerned a beautiful, deserving woman. What wouldn't she do to find an admirer! Under such circumstances, how can you blame a good-natured, cheerful woman who sits on the balcony, who tightens her corset, and who wears flashy colors and closely fitted boots; in short, who does any number of things that nobody would dare condemn as inherently evil or sinful because nothing is essentially wrong with them. In any case, she was perfectly justified. She wanted to marry, and rightfully so; there is nothing improper about that. She wanted to please someone, which is only natural, and marriage is the only known path. This is the path every woman takes; seldom, though, is there someone who can divine her thoughts. But we, however, shall enter into such details by describing to our readers everything that passed through Venturita's mind.

One day, Venturita's feet were highly praised. Her feet were often praised, but this time, the person who complimented them also happened to mention that . . . X, a rich and handsome youth, was very determined to see them as well.

That night, when Venturita was alone, she picked up one of the ankle boots she had worn that day. It retained the shape of her foot as though she were still wearing it. She examined its heel, instep, and uppers. Truly, hers was a sculptured foot, irreproachable, perfect; a foot that would stir the human soul; a foot, in brief, that was irresistible.

The following Sunday, Venturita went out in those ankle boots, and walked by the rows of young men with such dignity and nobility that no one would have suspected she was searching out of the corner of her eye for her special admirer. Nor would anyone have imagined that she had deliberately shortened the hem of her dress by an inch.

At last, she ran into her admirer not far from the Plaza de Iturbide. She saw him approach and (while pretending not to notice) was surprised by two looks that were like bolts of lightning, one directed at her eyes, and the other at her feet.

Venturita blessed those two bolts of lightning from the bottom of her heart, just as a farmer would—they meant the drought was ending.

That night, after examining her precious bronzed boot with an artistic eye and a deeply intuitive aesthetic, Venturita placed it on the marble surface of her dressing table and sank back into a gondola chair covered in red silk. She put her elbows on her knees and rested her chin on her folded hands as steadily as a marksman taking aim.

Here is Venturita face-to-face with her Krupp cannon, her machine gun, her torpedo—that is, with the most formidable attack weapon she had ever had within her reach. It would be truly impossible for a man not to go crazy over that boot, which formed the base . . . the base of a woman . . . yes, a woman not so worthless or advanced in years that . . . in short, it was the base of a marriageable young lady, for surely (as our readers have understood) Venturita was such a lady.

Venturita was resting at ease with her weapon before her. Like a conscientious soldier, she went over infantry tactics: she was ready for battle, equipped with a clean rifle, had plenty of ammunition, and kept her ear to the gunstock while looking at her commanding officer.

If we men were not as modest as we usually are, we would discover our true worth. If we considered the fact that there are thousands of girls advancing through the springtime of life who, like Venturita, have made a thorough study and formulated a strategic plan; who are, in short, manufacturing missiles to add to their arsenal of coquetries, all with the devious, yet entirely innocent, aim of seducing us, we would be quite proud.

Venturita, a prime example of these badly intentioned creatures, forswore no means and overlooked no possibilities. As we have seen, she set forth, valiantly and without reservations, on a tenacious struggle to achieve her ends, which were, without a doubt, perfectly legitimate and justifiable, as they concerned an unmarried, attractive woman who ran the imminent risk of becoming a perpetual sister-in-law.

We don't know how long Venturita contemplated her bronzed boot, but she was so absorbed in thought and immersed in medi-

tation that she didn't notice her best friend standing quietly behind her, waiting patiently to see how this solemn soliloquy regarding a hand-stitched, coquettish boot would end.

Venturita picked up her treasure once more by looping her right
forefinger and thumb through a small linen ribbon at the back.

Suspended from her slender, pink fingers, the ankle boot
rocked back and forth, pointing its tip toward the carpet. Before
Venturita's astonished eyes, it glittered with the red and gold
lights peculiar to this metallic shade of kid leather. Its shimmering rays were like the sparks from a sacred fire that is stirred by a
vestal virgin to keep it burning.

At that point, her friend could no longer contain her laughter.
Venturita, trembling from head to toe, let the boot fall and turned
around.

Every corner of the house echoed with the laughter that
poured forth from the lips of this joyful, vibrant young woman.

"Ventura!"

"Lola!"

"What are you doing, you naughty woman?"

"Nothing!"

"Nothing? You're up to something, and something big . . ."

"Don't be so wicked."

"I've been standing here for half an hour."

"And you've been watching me . . ."

"I've been watching you talk to your boot, the one I like so
much. It makes your foot look like a little girl's."

"Really? I've never had one that was so well made, and to think
that . . ."

"To think what?"

"Oh, nothing, to think that. . . . But don't leave. You're eating here today."

"That's impossible, my dear. I have to go shopping and—"

"No, no, tomorrow I'll go with you. But today I won't let you leave, I have too many things to tell you. Above all, I need to confide in you, I want to. . . . Close the door. You're the only person I can trust . . ."

". . . to watch you while you talk to your boots."

"That's right, to my boots. Don't laugh, Lola! You'll see—everything I said, you yourself have said a hundred times."

"How strange! But I don't talk to my . . ."

"Be quiet! Once you hear me, you'll agree."

Lola closed the door, took off her hat and coat and put them on the bed, then looked for her favorite little chair to pull up beside Venturita.

"Now then, let's see," Lola said, as she made herself comfortable in the chair. She arranged the pleats of her dress and ran her fingers up and down in that tactile inspection that the well-dressed woman performs so naturally and skillfully while straightening the lace on her dress and making sure she hasn't lost an earring.

"Yes, indeed," Venturita said, adopting a petulant tone. "I was talking to my boot, or more precisely, meditating on the subject of boots, which men consider to be one of our most irresistible attractions . . ."

"What do you mean, irresistible?" Lola said. "Not any more, my dear. Men are becoming more and more indifferent every day. Let me tell you what happened to me. A few days ago at my cousin's house, someone declared that he went mad over a pretty foot; he said an elegant foot made him lose all reason and enslaved him . . . in short, the man waxed eloquently on the subject. And I . . . I confess my sin: while he was speaking, I couldn't think of anything besides the new boots I was wearing."

"Those pretty ones you have on," Venturita interrupted.

"Yes, these ones," Lola replied, stretching her legs so that her perfectly shod feet extended beyond the hem of her dress. "Can you believe it? He saw them, and didn't say a word!"

"Are you sure he saw them?"

"Of course! In all their glory. I uncovered them and I'm certain he looked, but after that, nothing happened! My dear! It was as if he'd seen the feet of an Indian in huaraches!"*

"Something like that is happening to me! I also hoped to make a conquest with these boots. I wore them for the first time on Sunday with a definite purpose in mind, and not a thing happened. As far as I can tell, they've had no effect up to now. That's why I've been so lost in thought about the only recourse a poor woman has to make herself attractive and find a man who will make her happy. Let's see if you can guess, dear Lola, what that is. I've seen men running behind certain women . . . behind those women . . . you know, who aren't worth anything, while ignoring women of our category and class, even when we show ourselves off. I've run up my account at *La Sorpresa*, and when my brother-in-law finds out, there'll be trouble. I'm starting to wonder, Lola, if it's really true that fine shoes and pretty feet are among a woman's biggest charms."

"Of course they are, Ventura, of course! If you only knew what I know! My goodness! A man can lose himself over a pretty foot!"

"I confess that even though I'm not a man, I go delirious over the foot of a woman who is wearing proper shoes."

"With good reason, and I do, too. What's more, I can assure you, it's a taste shared by Mexican men."

"But I'm beginning to wonder. That's why I've been analyzing the shape of this boot: I want to understand why it attracts so much attention."

"And what have you learned from your meditations?"

"Well, many things, but don't laugh at me or call me pedantic if I talk about aesthetics."

"There you go again with your aesthetics! Ever since you became friends with that wise man who visits you so often, you talk about such strange things!"

"My friend has taught me many things. Take, for example, aesthetics. Here we have it applied to the boot. Of all the parts of the body, the human foot has the least appeal. A person should

* Traditional sandals worn by indigenous people.

be regarded from the ankle upwards, excluding the foot entirely. Greek and Roman matrons couldn't have been contemplated in any other way, because their toes and heels were displayed in such unsightly sandals. The refinement brought about by luxury and social manners was necessary to cover this human eyesore, and the art of the shoemaker reached its peak in the sumptuous court of Louis XV. Aesthetics embraced the shoe, and a lady's foot became one of the arrows used by Cupid to pierce men's hearts."

"Well said! Bravo, Ventura! Your wise friend has made you unrecognizable. But I still don't know what you mean by aesthetics."

"I'll explain. It means to correct the lines of Nature according to the principles of ideal beauty. For example, you may see a foot that's very ugly, but you can't explain why it's ugly."

"And you can?"

"Yes, I can."

"Explain it to me, then."

"Here we have a very ugly foot." And on the back of one of her calling cards, Venturita drew the outline of a foot using straight lines.

"Now I believe you—that foot is horrible," Lola said.

"And why is that?" Venturita continued, posing the question to herself. "It's because there are no curves; but if we force this foot, ugly as it is, to fit the conventional curves, we have the following."

And Venturita showed Lola her revised sketch.

"With only a slight correction made to the lines of the previous drawing, we now have a sculptured foot. When this same sculptured foot wears a shoe that was made twenty years ago, it looks horrible, yet if we take that horrible foot, and force it to follow the lines aesthetics has applied to the art of shoemaking, it looks like—"

"The eighth wonder of the world!" Lola exclaimed enthusiastically.

As can be seen, Venturita not only knew what kind of shoes to wear, but she also knew how to draw. Indeed, one might think she was an artist, and that Professor Corral* had been her teacher.

"You are a woman," Lola said, "who knows the principles behind things. Give me a kiss."

---

* A reference to Jesús Corral, a nineteenth-century Mexican painter and a professor of drawing at the Academia de San Carlos.

And Lola and Venturita leaned toward each other, searching for each other's lips, and . . . we don't want to explain why, but after they kissed they looked away in silence. This moment of silence was like the lightning that comes before the thunder.

This is how Venturita boomed:

"Lola, listen: even if they call me a coquette, even if they criticize me, I'm going to do it."

"What's that? What are you going to do?"

"Don't be surprised. I believe I have the perfect right to resort to any means."

"That's clear by now. I'd resort to them, too. What are you going to do?"

"Something very simple. On my morning walk this Sunday I'm not going to wear ankle boots: I'm going to wear shoes."

The blank look on Lola's face told Venturita that her friend was a very long way from understanding her.

"I can tell you're still a girl!" Venturita said.

"Why?"

"Because you haven't reacted to my plan."

"Explain it to me."

"Very well. Now listen patiently. A shoe is the weapon *par excellence*—it's our heavy artillery. If we regard flirtation as our missile, the shoe is . . . our dynamite."

"But Venturita—"

"Listen to me. With an ankle boot, you don't show anything besides your boot, but with a shoe, your stockings are revealed. Now do you understand?"

"Yes."

"Of course you understand! Stockings, my dear, stockings! In other words, a kind of nudity, an approach . . . a provocation . . . because stockings are something . . . something you should never show to anyone—they're your underclothes. Do you understand?"

"You know, you're right! I never thought of that."

"A foot," Venturita continued, "whose toes are barely enclosed by a silk shoe, and whose flesh can be discerned, or more precisely, can actually be seen through a lace stocking. . . . Oh, it's going too far, but I know very well what kind of influence a shoe can have on . . . on a woman's future. Now you understand why—" and

Venturita lowered her voice, "why those women —" and she lowered her voice even further, "wear that kind of shoe."

"My dear Venturita! So you're going to—"

"Yes, I am," Venturita replied, stamping her foot on the carpet. "I'm having a black satin pair made, and I'm going to wear them with silk stockings on Sunday. After all, everyone knows who I am, so they couldn't possibly confuse me with a. . . . But I'm going to do it, yes sir, I am, I'm determined to wear them."

Lola became very pensive, surprised that her friend had found such transcendence in subjects that seemed so simple.

It goes without saying that the two friends spoke of nothing else that day but aesthetics.

We return to Enriqueta.

As we have seen, Don Manuel had entered that home in good standing. He had picked up where others would have left off, by paying the rent. Enriqueta's mother still hadn't received any reply to her letters, and a few days later Don Manuel said good-bye while pressing a bill into her hands. Doña Dolores, who swallowed the shame such generosity causes, made coconut sweets the following day, which Don Manuel liked very much, and he took it upon himself to pay for some other urgent needs. Doña Dolores began to enjoy a certain domestic well-being, and one by one she added small comforts to her home. Her conscience was gradually put at ease by this formula for tranquillity:

"What would I do without Don Manuel?"

As for Enriqueta, if she didn't know as much as her mother did, she had some inkling about her future, for all young girls know when something is about to happen to them; but she didn't reveal it to anyone. She became slowly accustomed to Don Manuel and trusted him more and more, which was precisely what he was seeking. She trusted him so much, in fact, that one night she took the liberty of examining one of his rings, of which he had a very fine collection.

Don Manuel had been visiting them for some time now, and had yet to utter a single word about love. But he knew he had mastered the situation from the moment that (contrary to what we reported at the outset) Enriqueta no longer sat at the window while Don Manuel was there. Now it was Doña Lola who excused herself, saying that she needed more light to sew or had some errands to do (which, understandably, became more complicated as the days went by), leaving her daughter alone with Don Manuel so that they could talk freely.

The author is not unaware of Doña Dolores's repugnant behavior, and it is not by choice that he draws this scene. Unfortunately, such arrangements exist, and not only do they exist, but they have multiplied throughout Mexico City, much to the detriment of morality and good habits. The invasion of luxury into the middle class has led more and more to their downfall every day, and we know many mothers who are living under the same roof with a daughter who has the social position of a courtesan.

Doña Dolores had brought her daughter to Mexico City for the same reason that the Indians bring their best fruit, to be consumed, and that was because the father, mother, and daughter did not form a family, which is the supreme law of morality. Doña Dolores was the pot in which the flower had been sown; Enriqueta's papa had been the gardener; and Enriqueta had arrived in the world like a product for the market. Those pure bonds of affection that we have toward the authors of our days were, in Enriqueta's heart, replaced by a vague idea of her father, who was the husband of another woman and the father of other children. He had strayed from the path with Doña Dolores who, as we know, belonged to the lowest ranks. As a consequence, everything Doña Dolores did seemed bad to Enriqueta, who secretly, and with more than enough reason, called her mother vulgar.

Filial respect, and the tender and blessed veneration a child feels for his mother, are like the petals stirring on a young bud that will soon open and release the treasures of its perfume into the atmosphere.

When a mother is loved, respected, and venerated, virtue will find a place in a child's heart.

These low-class girls who fancy themselves elegant, these upstarts in bustles who powder their face, sport Louis XV heels, and wear their hair in bangs, who can be seen walking with their mother in tow, a poor, good-natured wretch who looks more like her daughter's seamstress, believe they have come so far that they can scorn the authors of their days; yet these young ladies, civilized and poor, run a greater risk of being easy game for the man-about-town than of becoming wives.

Virtuous daughters are born to be mothers; the others are born to be "kept."

Enriqueta's destiny could have been foretold.

She was being kept by Don Manuel at the same time we have reason to mention her, for she was one of the "real beauties" Saldaña spoke about.

V I

How the Appearances Maintained by These Upstarts Tend to Compromise Any Serious Result

Only two months had gone by since a young man arrived in Mexico City, fresh from his tour of Europe and the United States upon completing his studies in one of the best schools in Germany. He was traveling to educate himself and to learn as much about the world as his considerable fortune would allow. He had been gone four years, and the Republic of Mexico was one of the final stops on his itinerary before he returned to Venezuela, his native country. Enrique Pérez Soto (as our new character is named) was acquainted with luxury and beauty; he was a man from the most select society who observed the rules of etiquette and followed every social custom. Because of all he had seen as a young man, he was no longer very impressionable; but like all *touristes*, he kept searching for one more impression.

In his last letter to his family, which he wrote after much hesitation, he announced that he had chosen to stay in Mexico much longer than he had calculated in his travel plan for the Americas.

It so happened that, for the first time in his life, Enrique fell truly and positively in love; and however much he made fun of himself during those two months, he could not deny, in his moments of deep reflection, that his little "Mexicana" (which is what he called her, as he hadn't learned her name yet) had impressed him deeply.

Enrique Pérez greatly enjoyed what he called the game of Mexican courtship. He didn't miss a single Sunday at the Zócalo, where he would watch her as she passed by three or four times in that exploratory stroll favored by women, in which they take a turn around the garden between rows of young dandies and bearded gentlemen who stand on either side, making a choice or passing judgment on what is available.

Enrique also saw his little "Mexicana" on weekday afternoons, when she was usually sitting in the Alameda Park on one of the benches facing the Church of the Corpus Christi.

One day a friend told him, "I think you're making too great an effort to contemplate that beauty."

"You're right. I've had the same thought, but I confess, that woman has made a vivid impression on me. More than anything else, I'm captivated by her eyes."

"That's what you've been telling me for the past two months, but you still don't know who she is."

"I've decided I don't want to know."

"How strange. Why is that?"

"For the same reason I don't look at my lottery tickets until the last minute: I want to keep my hopes up."

"If that's true, then you're in no danger. But I wouldn't like it if you fell in love, so I'm going to investigate. Maybe you'll become disenchanted as a result."

"Don't do that. Let me adore my Mexican girl from afar. Look, here she comes! What a waist! What lovely feet! How beautifully she dresses! She's a queen!"

At that moment she walked by and brushed against Enrique's arm. She saw him all over town and knew that he was he was pursuing her, however inoffensively. For some time now, she was in the habit of bestowing a smile upon him, so imperceptibly done that only Enrique's eye could appreciate the contraction of her upper lip. This small gesture made her admirer shiver with pleasure.

After she passed by, Enrique stopped his friend and made him turn around so that they could walk in the footsteps of his quarry.

"Which one is she?"

"The one who smiled. Didn't you see her?"

"No, I must have been looking at the other girl, who wasn't smiling. Who is she?"

"I believe it's her sister."

"But they don't look alike. And that's where your fears should begin."

"Why?"

"I'll tell you why. Never trust a family with children who don't look alike."

"What! There you go on one of your—"

"The reason is clear. In these godforsaken places you'll find families with several papas and mamas, and . . ."

"Look," Enrique interrupted. "They're sitting down. There's some room on the next bench; let's take a seat."

The two friends hastened their step, and after passing in front of the two sisters, who had already sat down, they claimed the neighboring bench.

"Good afternoon." They were greeted by a man already sitting there.

"Good afternoon," Enrique's friend replied.

"How are you? What have you been doing?"

"Nothing, as you can see. We're getting some fresh air."

"And looking at girls."

"Naturally."

"And it seems, my friend, that you're an expert on the subject."

"Enrique, let me introduce you to Señor Jiménez, a great connoisseur of society, and a man with excellent connections."

"At your service," Jiménez said.

"Enrique Pérez Soto. Pleased to meet you . . ." Enrique answered.

"Señor Jiménez knows everyone in Mexico City," Enrique's friend continued.

"Were you born in the capital?" Enrique asked.

"Yes, indeed."

"I'll bet you know our neighbors."

"What neighbors?"

"The ones on our right."

"Ah, those two young girls!"

"Yes, the ones wearing white hats."

"Ah, yes! Of course."

"Who are they?"

"One is named Leonor, and the other is Gumesinda."

"You see?" Enrique's friend told him. "It would have been materially impossible for Señor Jiménez not to have known them. Now, what other details can you provide, if we're not being too indiscreet . . ."

"I have no objection to telling you whatever I know."

"Good; now, if you would be so kind . . . because . . . let's be frank. My friend Enrique is hopelessly in love with one of them."

"Which one?" Jiménez immediately asked.

"The taller girl," Enrique said, as though he were seeking approval for his choice.

"I'm very glad," Jiménez answered.

"Oh? That means . . . ?" Enrique's friend added maliciously.

"Yes, how can I deny it? I've got something for Gumesinda."

"They seem to be well off," Enrique said.

"I don't believe they're very rich," Jiménez answered.

"Who provides for them?"

"Their brother, the paymaster Machuca, supports them."

"Oh! So they're Machucas!"

"Listen, chum," Enrique's friend said. "You must admit, their last name is hardly poetic. Petrarch wouldn't have written a single sonnet to Laura if her last name had been Machuca. You'd better get used to calling her Leonor, which is another matter, and don't try to change her last name to your more euphonious one."

Instead of answering, Enrique bit his lip.

"Well, then," Enrique's friend continued, addressing Jiménez, "at what stage are your affections?"

"I'm simply an admirer," Jiménez answered, somewhat despondently. "But I have reason to believe the situation will change for the better next Saturday."

"Why?"

"I've been invited to a ball and the Machucas will be there."

"You lucky fellow!" Enrique exclaimed, clapping his hands together.

"Well, perhaps you'd like . . ."

"Like to what?"

"Go to the ball."

"Me! Go to the ball! But . . . are you . . . ?"

"Of course. I'm authorized to invite my friends."

"That would make me the happiest man on earth."

"I'll bring both of you."

"I accept. Where shall we meet?" Enrique asked.

"I'll pick you up . . ."

"At the Hotel de San Carlos," Enrique and his friend said in unison.

"At nine o'clock on Saturday night."

"Agreed. Thanks a million, Señor Jiménez. We'll go to the ball, and no doubt we'll find someone who will introduce us to—to—"

"To the Machucas," Enrique's friend added. "Don't be tonguetied; you'd better get used to your sweetheart's horrendous name as soon as possible. Machuca! That brings such unpoetic images to mind: aah—aah—choo!"

"Don't be so cruel, my friend!" Enrique implored. "No matter how much you laugh, Señor Jiménez and I are proud to be completely under their influence."

"Indeed," Jiménez said.

"And of course," Enrique added in a hushed tone, "you'll introduce us, and we'll dance, and—"

"Naturally," Jiménez said, "and I've decided to make a full declaration of my love, but—"

"What?" Enrique asked.

"I have my tactics. I never declare my love during the first few dances."

"You don't?"

"I wait until the drinks have been passed around, and since that girl knows how to down them—"

"Yes, sir!" Enrique's friend exclaimed. "Alcohol is a first-rate assistant to a man in love. As soon as the young maiden he desires is half-loaded, he waits for his 'yes.'"

"You make fun of everything," Enrique said, annoyed. "The truth is, since there are only two Machucas, you've been left empty-handed."

"But I'll have a good laugh watching the two of you set off on your conquests."

"Excuse me," Jiménez interrupted. "There are three Machucas."

"Wonderful, my boy, that's wonderful!" Enrique said. "Why don't you try your luck with the third, even if she's named Machuca."

"And she's the prettiest," Jiménez added.

"What did you say?"

"I said she's not half-bad. In any case, we each have a Machuca."

"Ah, yes, we three . . . But now they're leaving . . . they're standing up . . . here they come."

And indeed Leonor and Gumesinda walked by, turning their faces quite naturally toward the three young men. Leonor smiled at Enrique once more in farewell. He doffed his hat with a great flourish, and the sisters nodded in return.

"Magnificent!" exclaimed Jiménez, rubbing his hands. "They've taken the bait. That greeting marks the beginning of our friendship. Now I can't wait for Saturday to arrive."

"If I may say so," Enrique's friend turned to Jiménez, "I hope your impatience doesn't lead you to declare your love before those drinks are served."

"Your strategy is excellent," Enrique said, "but I'd rather not attribute my success to the influence of wine. I'd prefer . . ."

"Oh, yes! A clean conquest, a heroic victory," Jiménez said.

"It's far more satisfying. Moreover, we might very well discover, and in fact it's quite probable, that those young ladies don't drink . . . "

"What do you mean!" Jiménez exclaimed. "I have my sources. I've been told by a reliable informant that—"

"Yes?" the two friends asked together, coming to a stop and leaning closer to Jiménez.

"Well, my friends, the truth about Leonor . . ."

"What's that?"

"She drinks like a fish."

"A drunkard! Tsk, tsk," said Enrique's friend, laughing uproariously.

As soon as Enrique parted from his friends he felt, like all lovers, the need to be alone. This need illustrates the dual nature of love: one either wishes to be with the object of one's affections, or by one's self, eliminating all other influences.

That afternoon Enrique had collected two smiles, and then following those two smiles, a greeting. All together, they were like the first three rays of sunshine in a day full of light and poetry. Such a day represents, in a lover's imagination, the culmination of his illusion, because whatever pleasures may follow, nothing compares to that first instant.

Those were Enrique's feelings, and his joy wouldn't fit inside his chest. He needed solitude and shade in order to savor it. It was one of those moments in which heroic lovers are born: he had already closed his eyes to any objection, any difficulty, any obstacle that would steer him from his path. Enrique felt he could do anything; he would accept the greatest of sacrifices and submit to the harshest of tests; that is, he would perform courageous and valiant deeds if that were the only way he could attain the object of his desire.

Despite his exultant mood, his friend's mockery of the Machucas reverberated within the realm of his fantasy, since it is well known that the number one enemy of love is ridicule.

"Machuca!" Enrique repeated. "What a shame their last name is Machuca! But if you come right down to it, the last name doesn't make a difference. On the other hand, her first name is poetic. Leonor! Oh! Leonor! And what about the other thing Jiménez said, that the Machucas are fond of the bottle . . . how awful! But he must be exaggerating. Surely he means that Leonor enjoys sampling fine wines and tasting fine delicacies. That's it! It's really a recommendation. Yes, without a doubt. How could this beautiful woman, who carries herself so gracefully, and with such a distinguished air, have such a repugnant flaw as drunkenness! No. What nonsense! Jiménez, like everyone else, likes to spread gossip about others. Whatever the case, I am deeply in love with Leonor—against my will, it's true, but I couldn't imagine living without her. What can I do? My chance has come and . . . forward march! The happiness of my entire life is bound up in one word: Leonor! and there's no one who can dissuade me. In fact, I think I'll write her a letter, which she'll receive today, and then this Saturday at the ball, during the first number we dance together . . . oh, what joy! I imagine her saying 'yes,' and then we'll hold hands, and I'll squeeze her waist, and . . . I'll devour her with my eyes . . . and it will be . . . heavenly! Love, at the height of its power, subjugating two hearts destined to beat forever as one!"

Enrique rubbed his hands, stood up, and looked at himself in the mirror. For a few minutes he gesticulated like a madman as he paced the floor of his room. Finally, he sat in the chair at his writing table.

"Leonor," he wrote on a piece of note paper. "Leonor? Isn't that a little too informal? I'll call her Leonor when . . . but in my first letter . . ." He took another piece of paper:

Dear Miss Machuca,
This afternoon I could hardly contain myself, and I greeted you at the risk of appearing too forward; but . . .

"But why? What excuse can I offer? Aha! I've thought of a good one!"

. . . but you know, you know how long I have known you, followed you, watched you, admired you, and . . . loved you.

"That's a good opening; above all, it's natural— or realist, as they say nowadays. After reading it, she'll have no choice but to continue."

Please don't think that I am enchanted by your beauty alone. At first, I myself would have said so; but I have decided to write to you today because I deeply believe that I have come to love you with the truest passion and the most intense feeling; and it is with the most unshakable resolve that I desire to unite my destiny to yours for eternity. I am single; I am rich; and I am a gentleman. This Saturday, at the Colonel's ball, you will tell me if I am destined to be the happiest, or most unfortunate, man on earth.

"Magnificent!" Enrique exclaimed, sealing the letter and putting it in his pocket. He grabbed his hat and left the room. While Enrique looks for a way to have his letter delivered into Leonor's hands, we will take a quick glance at the characters who were preparing for Saldaña's ball at that very moment.

Not surprisingly, there was no acquaintance of the Machuca sisters who was not directly, indirectly, or surreptitiously vested with the right to attend. If there had been more days left before the ball, the informality and *sans façon* of these invitations would have resulted in a formidable eruption at the Colonel's house, as each guest followed the well-known practice of inviting a hundred more.

The girls who took the waters at the Pane Baths, along with their three admirers and two aspiring admirers; Enriqueta, Don Manuel's mistress, with a new dress and flashy boots, accompanied by her entertaining young friend who, thanks to the loan of a frock coat, would look almost elegant; Saldaña, with the "mother of his little ones," and a friend who was escorting her in his stead; the notary and his wife and daughters; the four dandies who played billiards near the Plaza de Iturbide; the clerk at the House of Lohse; Jiménez, Enrique, and Enrique's friend; and finally, Venturita and Lola, who had somehow been invited, by what means no one knew, perhaps because Venturita's brother-in-law had some dealings with Saldaña; and we haven't taken into account the fact that the Colonel had invited a general and a major, as well as two or three officers on leave who, in his opinion, cut the best figure and had the finest manners in the corps.

We also have Camacho and his lady friend, who was Saldaña's first choice; the general who was drinking his chocolate in the Concordia; the government official who found Saldaña to be so useful; and Peña and other assorted people, among them Don Quintín, whom Saldaña had persuaded over a glass of sherry to throw caution to the wind.

The musicians had been auditioned and hired. The band consisted of a large double bass, which was difficult to carry, and even more difficult to maneuver through the curtained doorway to its assigned corner. Behind the double bass came three brass instruments: a tuba, a trombone, and, most important, a trumpet, which would speak the loudest, or at least would startle the audience the greatest; and lastly, two violins and a flute.

Ever since Friday, Saldaña, assisted by Doña Bartola, the Colonel, and Matilde, had been busy putting candles in the chandeliers and candelabras, and the house began to fill up with furniture, housewares, and crates.

Doña Bartola received the dress she intended to wear on the night of the ball. It was entirely of her own design, but its creation was the work of her dressmaker.

The dress was made of satin and had an indefinable color, somewhere between mocha and cranberry and verging on rust; this color didn't belong to the family of reds, but was of clear descent. It contained enough yellow to make it seem neither red nor brown; and it wavered hesitantly toward leaf green. In any case, no one could say what color the dress was. After contemplating this neutral and impossible shade, the dressmaker wasn't able to find any ornaments that matched, so she used enameled beads of a thousand different colors which, in combination, formed a veritable riot of indescribable lights. She knew that the lady who ordered the dress was named Bartola, and that these beads would create a great sensation. Indeed, the dress (which weighed ten pounds) radiated every imaginable color; it lit up like a chandelier and sparkled with the rarest tints and the most incredible hues.

Saldaña and Doña Bartola's husband were amazed, and agreed that she would look dazzling at the ball, for the dress appeared to be arrayed in diamonds.

However, the mother whose daughters went to the Pane Baths had to send a servant to the pawnshop ("to the bank" as she put it) in order to meet some of her daughters' minor expenses. It was only through this type of sacrifice that the girls were able to show themselves in public during hard times.

The Ball Begins

Saldaña ate lunch and dinner at the Colonel's house almost every day that week, but because of all there was to do on Saturday, he needed to be on duty from breakfast on, assisting with the delivery of liquor from Don Quintín and receiving the chairs, silverware, plates, and other rented items.

Saldaña rearranged the furniture, improvised tables in the dining room, and placed serving dishes, glasses, and silverware all around. He commissioned the Colonel to slice the Gruyère cheese; directed a captain to open the sardine tins; and called upon Doña Bartola to arrange the olives on crystal platters. In the meantime, he built pyramids out of the pastries and cakes, and distributed the bottles of liquor with a certain strategy and forethought.

"What are you doing, Saldaña?" the Colonel asked.

"You see, Colonel, I'm an expert in these matters. You must agree, not everyone knows about liquor. Everyone drinks, that's true, but even those who call themselves connoisseurs can be fooled by a cheap imitation. For example, here you have a sickly sweet, fake sherry in a beautiful bottle. That's for the ladies, as are the malaga wine and the muscatel. And here you have some cheap champagne for the communion of martyrs, which is served to create noise and fill the dining room with the sound of popping corks. But come over this way, Colonel. See this crate? That's the Santa Barbara! And here's a cognac that's been aged for thirty years, along with some Hungarian wine, an authentic sherry, and the finest champagne, of the Viuda e Imperial label. So whenever you'd like to invite a special friend into the dining room for a drink, let me know. I'm the only one who knows where these are hidden. Understand, Colonel? Now, as far as the pastries are concerned, there are some for the troops and some for the officers. I'm the only one who can tell the difference, because from the outside they all look the same. But these cost only one peso per hundred, while the others are three times the price."

"But my good fellow," the Colonel interrupted. "I think there's too much."

"Too much of what?"

"Too much to drink and too much of everything."

"You don't know how people are. You'll see, it'll all disappear like magic. In my opinion, there can never be too much. I've even given a little something to Don Quintín's assistant so that no matter the hour, he'll send us more supplies if the need arises. I always plan ahead."

Saldaña had not only taken charge of the provisions, but had also reinforced the kitchen staff to help wash the plates and glasses. As a result, at five o'clock that afternoon the domain of the cook was invaded by a tribe of pot scrubbers.

With only a few hours to go before the ball, the Colonel, Doña Bartola, and Matilde all had swollen feet.

Leonor received the letter from Enrique, or, rather, from the elegant young man who had greeted her in the park, whose name she still didn't know. She paid no attention to the letter's sincerity; what most struck her was the sentence, "I am rich."

The happy times that have made the Mexican woman a model wife are fast disappearing. The invasion of luxury into the lower classes has muddied the pure wellsprings of domestic virtue, turning modesty and humility into an insatiable desire for fancy baubles to deceive society with a wealth and comfort that do not exist.

Led on by these new yearnings, women have chosen to stand at the brink of a precipice, for they believe they have discovered something superior to virtue in the real world.

As soon as she received Enrique's letter, Leonor began to make inquiries, and Jiménez (by way of Gumesinda) was asked to be her informant. Jiménez praised Enrique to the skies, exaggerating his fortune above all else. Without prying any further, Leonor decided to make the definitive conquest at the ball.

A woman from the ground floor of the building where the mother of Saldaña's children lived had put herself in charge of her neighbor's toilette. She placed on top of a table (the only one in the room) an old sardine tin filled with water from the cistern, a scrub brush made from the fibers of a maguey plant, and a comb with only a few teeth left.

As the poor, modest, and unassuming mother of Saldaña's children, Lupe had never thought of covering her forehead with bangs: she kept her brow plain and simple so that all could see the traces of her sadness, which showed in certain lines that were only visible when she laughed or cried.

This neighbor gave off airs of elegance because she went to Sunday Mass wearing a Spanish mantilla and was among the few whose hair was cut in a "fringe." The first thing she did to Lupe's hair was lop it off in front.

After this tonsure, there stood up on Lupe's forehead something that looked like a paintbrush dipped in ocote pine resin. Her hair, besides having a very pronounced black cowlick, was as rebellious as the maguey bristles of the scrub brush. Between the scrub brush, the paintbrush, Lupe, and her neighbor, a veritable

battle was waged. The water in the sardine tin was emptied twice, and the victim's scalp began to show the effects of this treatment. An emollient was needed. The neighbor sent a boy to the barber shop down the street to ask Don Carmen for a small amount of lemon or cinnamon-scented pomade.

A short while later the boy returned, waving the *Opoponax* which Don Carmen, lacking any other means, had wrapped in paper.

The pomade wasn't strong enough to tame Lupe's rebellious mane, which had been accustomed to its weight for some twenty-odd years. There was no way to make her bangs lie flat as God willed it, or to force them to fall by their own weight above her eyebrows. After being smoothed down, her hair would immediately stand up again and part to either side, obeying its old habits.

In the end, it was necessary to resort to the test of fire. The neighbor sent the boy to Doña Antonia, the washerwoman who lived in number 7, to borrow her curling iron. After heating the iron, the neighbor broke (or, more precisely, scorched) those mutinous bangs that refused to lie down above Lupe's eyebrows.

Lupe got up from this rack of torture and looked into a broken-off mirror. She couldn't recognize herself. She looked so different that not even the father of her little ones would have known her.

Lupe's corset, a seldom-used object in her trunk, was taken out by its rusty hooks. By making the necessary tucks, it served to improve the lines given her by Mother Nature; and with this change, the blue dress from the pawnshop fell into place.

Lupe's complexion was not so dark that it couldn't benefit from a touch of cosmetics. After her neighbor applied a thick layer of powder, it seemed as if Lupe had sprung to life like Pygmalion's statue and stepped down from the pedestal. She was rejuvenated and looked elegant, in sharp contrast to the room, its furnishings, and Saldaña's little ones.

Once the dress was fitted, Lupe's neighbor went back to her quarters to find an artificial flower already used by several other neighbors who, like Lupe, had been invited to a ball.

Meanwhile, Lupe's children opened their eyes wide, hardly understanding their mother's strange transformation. The boy who went for the pomade held up a tallow candle to illuminate this portrait. Neighbors converged at the half-open door, attracted by the novelty.

As soon as the neighbor in charge of Lupe's toilette placed the artificial flower in her hair, she opened the door to let the curious onlookers inside.

"Come in, Doña Margarita. Come in, everyone," she said to the women at the door.

The room was invaded by six neighbors.

"Oh, what a lovely little dress! It's pure silk!"

"And made by a dressmaker!"

"You can tell *that* a block away. Have you ever seen such perfect pleats?"

"I'm sure many fancy ladies will be there, but no one will be wearing a finer dress than yours, Doña Gualupita."

"Aren't those bangs cute, Doña Anita?"

"You see, sweetie? It's what I've been telling you: cut your hair. These days only poor girls keep it long."

A girl sat on the floor to analyze and touch what she called Lupe's "underthings."

"Let's see her feet," several women said.

The boy who was holding the candle placed it on the floor, and the examination now passed from head to foot.

"It's bronzed kidskin and patent leather."

"What lovely feet she has!"

"There's nothing like quality! What a change from those worn-out shoes she usually wears! They're beautiful. Is it real kidskin?"

"Yes, it's real," Lupe answered, filled with a satisfaction she couldn't hide.

Another neighbor raised Lupe's skirt and inspected the decoration on her petticoats.

"Embroidery like that costs up to one and a half reales a yard."

"Not any longer, Doña Anita, I found some for only one real."

These inquisitive women would have stared at Lupe all night if Saldaña's friend, her escort to the ball, hadn't appeared on the scene.

"Good evening."

"Good evening, Don Lucio," said the neighbor who fixed Lupe's hair.

"Good ev'ning t'you, sir," an old woman said. "Come in."

"Good evening," the rest of the neighbors said in unison.

Once again the boy lifted his candle high, certain that the visitor would want to contemplate Lupe.

"You look so elegant," the newcomer exclaimed. "You're like another woman."

"Isn't that true, Don Lucio? She's a picture to behold."

"Good Lord!" an old woman said. "Look what a few rags can do! It's not for nothing young girls go crazy over clothes these days."

"There's nothing like money."

"That's for sure," one of the neighbors added. "Money makes the dog dance."

"But Don Saldaña is rich," said another maliciously.

"Oh, yes!" added a third. "Whenever he comes here for lunch he buys turkey with mole sauce and spends a few reales on pulque."

"That's true, but I was thinking about the dress."

"That dress must have cost a few pesos."

"Of course! It's pure silk!"

"And it's the best kind, because some silks cost as little as six reales, but not this silk."

"You'd better go, dearie, it's getting late. It's long past eight o'-clock," one of the women said.

"Whenever you're ready," Don Lucio said.

This Don Lucio, Saldaña's friend, was wearing a buttoned-up black frock coat and a top hat. He kept his hat on so that the neighbors could study it to their heart's content.

Don Lucio would blend in perfectly with the guests at the ball. From his appearance alone, no one would suspect he was an artist, that is, an artist of hair styling with his own salon or, in other words, that he was a barber. Since his barber shop measured only ten feet wide and was located on a distant street, Saldaña was sure no one would recognize him at the ball.

Once Lupe was perfectly attired and had been inspected by her neighbors, she put a black stole over her shoulders and carefully covered her hair with a white woolen scarf. After leaving her children in the care of a neighbor, she closed the door to her quarters and, lifting her blue skirt with both hands, tiptoed down the uneven pavement of the patio toward the front gate. Her audience accompanied her and kindly lit up the way with several tallow candles. Two boys held up matches to light the alley as Lupe stepped by.

At last she reached the sidewalk on the arm of her escort, and was on her way to the ball.

At eight o'clock that evening, Saldaña began to light the candles in the salon, while Matilde, Bartolita, and her husband attended to their toilette. The kitchen was crowded with servants who had seen each other for the first time that day.

"I don't know if we can leave now," said a pot scrubber whose head was covered with a tattered rebozo. "A whole day washin' dishes, and my clothes, they're all soak'd."

"My hands are so worn, my blood's about to burst," said another of the same trade. "But they haven't paid us, so I think they still need us."

"What for?"

"What d'you mean, what for? For washin'."

"The floors?"

"No, the dishes."

"They're not clean yet?"

"Wait 'til those young devils get here, and you'll see what a mess they make. I know what I'm talkin' about."

"If that's why we're here, then it's a whole diff'rent song, isn't it, Doña?"

"They'll pay us extra, for keepin' us awake all night . . . don't you think?"

"They ain't giv'n us enough for a swig of pulque."

"Thank God I spent three *tlacos** on my own."

* A coin of very little value.

"Bless you! I came here wi' no money, I was in such a hurry."

"So you're thirsty, are you?" The youngest man on the kitchen staff posed this question with a certain erotic intention. He drew closer to the two pot scrubbers, who had been holding their conversation while kneeling on the floor in the posture of Aztec idols.

"Ooh no!" the more bashful of the two said, moving her head coquettishly while wrapping her rebozo around to conceal her mouth.

When a lady and a gentleman flirt, Cupid teases them with a brooch that seems ready to fall off, and with a lacy cuff turned inside out; with a lady's fan that stops opening when certain words are uttered, and with rosy fingertips that assume the position of a butterfly's antennae. That is, Cupid plays with smiles and gazes, with innuendoes and broken-off sentences, and even with sighs. But when we speak of love among our servant class, then Cupid, the lacy cuff, the fan, the smile, and the rest are all forgotten. Instead, a pair of hands held close to the face open the rebozo halfway to allow a quick glimpse of a coppery neck, then it is wrapped around again to cover the mouth a little bit more, even when the weather's not cold. Her admirer eloquently translates this gesture to mean: "Behave yourself," "I'm very shy," "That make me blush," etc., etc.

If the pot scrubber had simply said that she was or wasn't thirsty, the servant would have turned away with indifference; but since she had said, "Ooh no!" and hid her face in her rebozo, he understood, at that supreme moment, the immensity of his good fortune.

In order to hasten its progress, he approached one of his comrades, a servant in Saldaña's trust.

"Hey chief," he said in a guarded tone. "The ladies say they're thirsty."

"What ladies?"

"The ones washin' the dishes."

"So?"

"I'm tellin' you because, you'll see, the servants'll get the dregs later on, or they won't get nothin' at all."

"But Don Saldaña put me in charge, and I don't want 'em to say . . ."

"But what can he say! How'll he miss one bottle?"

"Well . . . ," the hired man said, scratching his head. "What you need to do is guess where . . ."

"Look . . . can it be true? How'd this li'l bottle find its way into the straw?" the servant said after leading his friend to a crate in an inner patio.

"Anisette!" his companion said, holding it up to the light coming from the kitchen. "Well, since it's anisette, take it to the ladies."

The lucky winner poured half his prize into a pitcher, then stuck the bottle back in the straw again. He went to the kitchen in search of the pot scrubbers, who in the meantime had fallen asleep while sitting on the floor.

"Go on," he said to the woman who had wrapped herself in the rebozo.

"Go on" is a time-honored expression used by cavaliers of the serape; "go on" means "Have a drink," or "Drink up," or "It's on me," etc., etc.

The pot scrubber thus favored took the pitcher by its rim, placed three fingers inside, and passed it to her companion, repeating, "Go on."

Her companion's nose, eyes, and forehead disappeared into the pitcher. Losing herself in the anisette, she inhaled deeply and drank it with great gusto. She passed the pitcher back to her friend, who returned it to the host. He refused to take it from her, and repeated the sacramental phrase "go on."

The pot scrubber downed the anisette, and without looking at her benefactor, handed the pitcher back to him. She used her rebozo to wipe her lips, and demurely covered her mouth once again.

He went to the inner patio.

None of this went unnoticed by the other servants, especially Francisca, whose eye had been on this cupbearer all day long. She looked for an excuse to run into him in the patio.

"I've got somethin' for you, Doña Pachita," he said.

"What?"

"A li'l anisette. I knew how those women'd talk, so I gave 'em a swig."

"Ah! I t'ought you was . . ."

"Go on, Doña Pachita," he repeated, stretching the pitcher over to her.

"You think I'm goin' to drink anisette, after that. . . . Well, why not!"

Francisca made a face as she drank it, then returned to the kitchen. Three ingredients were already in place for the ensuing fermentation: love, jealousy, and anisette.

In the meantime, Saldaña had finished lighting all the candles. The musicians arrived, speaking very softly and slipping quietly one after the other into the house. Saldaña showed them to the room next to the salon, and then went to the kitchen to continue his preparations.

The house was completely silent, and a damp air redolent of wet bricks permeated the rooms. A double row of petroleum lamps had been placed in the doorway, patio, and stairway. Everything was lit up, clean, and ready to receive the guests.

At half-past eight, a head covered in white brightened the hallway amid the flowerpots. She was the first guest to enter the house and, surprised by the silence that reigned there, was afraid she had made some mistake.

"This can't be it!"

"Yes, it's here," her escort said. "I know this house like the back of my hand. It's a fancy ball, so the guests are coming late. Let's go inside."

The lady and her escort paused a moment at the doorway and entered the salon. After looking all around, they satisfied themselves that they were the first to arrive.

"There's no one here," she said quietly.

"It's better this way—we don't have to greet anyone. Have a seat."

The lady sat down without removing her head covering, since it seemed more fitting to keep that white cloth on her head. Her companion sat in the next chair and put his hat beside him. After a few moments of silence, they began to comment upon the salon and its furniture.

After some time passed, other women arrived, and as there was no one to receive them, they entered on their own, because that was why they came, to make an entrance, and as there was a lady already there, they headed toward her.

This lady was none other than Lupe, the mother of Saldaña's little ones. The new arrivals placed the fingertips of their right hand on her left shoulder and murmured "Good evening," or "How are you?" more distractedly than attentively. After making this gesture, each lady immediately sat down, and when six of them had taken seats, more ladies arrived, who then repeated this business of placing their fingertips on each other's shoulders before finding an empty chair. No two were acquainted, so their would-be embraces and greetings such as "How are you?" and "Good evening" became more and more lackluster, to the point that these women didn't greet each other as much as sniff each other. Indeed, this ritual was more canine than social. When there were ten ladies assembled, the next ones to arrive were not as eager to embrace each and every one, and so after reaching the fifth or sixth in line, they merely nodded their heads and sat down.

All the men stayed in the vestibule and the hallway. The young dandies thrust their hands into white gloves, acting more like boxers than dancers. One of them exclaimed:

"What the heck, I'm going to kick up my heels tonight!"

"Me, too, but don't be selfish! You know all the girls, so find me a partner."

"Are the Machucas here yet?" one of the dandies asked, standing on tiptoe.

"No, they're coming later," another answered, presuming to know their plans.

By now so many people had arrived that the musicians decided it was time to tune their instruments. The flute burst forth with a piercing *la*, and the double bass breathed like a lion smelling meat. The flesh of the young men began to tremble with anticipation and excitement.

Bartolita, her husband, and Matilde hadn't appeared yet; they had so many things to do while getting dressed. The flute, however, sounded a note of warning.

More than twenty people were in the salon, and the hosts still weren't ready. Bartolita's husband was the first to come out of his bedroom, limping.

"What's the matter, Colonel?" Saldaña asked, noticing that the Colonel had to lean on chairs as he walked.

"What is it? That damned shoemaker made these boots too tight!"

"They're boots for dancing, Colonel, dancing. They give your feet such an elegant line."

"I don't give a hoot about elegance! I can't even walk!"

"They'll stretch if you take a few steps."

"I don't think I can break them in."

"Let your feet get used to them."

"And what about my wife? Where is she? Is she in the salon?"

"No, she's getting dressed."

"Dear God! It's taking her so long! The guests are by themselves."

"If you think it's a good idea, I'll have the musicians play something to keep them entertained. That way they won't miss their hosts."

"Very well, let them play."

Saldaña entered the salon and went into the side room where the musicians were.

"Maestro, play us some music. It's time to begin."

The double bass was slowly stood upright, and the musicians finished tuning their instruments.

Saldaña noticed that many of the ladies still had their coats on, and he went around urging them to take them off. His left arm became piled with shawls, jackets, theater wraps, scarves, and capes, forming a promontory that could barely fit through the doorway. He took his load to a bedroom, and flipped everything onto a bed. In so doing, he set the stage for the coats to be mixed up and lost.

There were also hats, canes, frock coats, and umbrellas lying on top of tables and chairs. Saldaña collected these articles and added them to the pile on the bed in order to clear the salon.

The music began. It was a polka, but hardly anyone realized it. Lupe and those of her kind couldn't dance the polka, much less Don Lucio. And the young men were the sort who don't attend dancing school, as these are few and far between in this cultured city, but who nonetheless spring into action with an intuitive choreography that comes with their age and audacity. It is easiest for them to learn the habanera, which is hardly a dance, being little more than a swaying and touching to the beat.

There was no one, then, who could dance the polka. Saldaña appealed to the men:

"Gentlemen, how about a polka."

"I can't dance the polka."

"Me neither."

"Have them play an habanera."

"Yes, that's better."

"Maestro, an habanera," Saldaña whispered in the ear of the violin player. Enrique, Jiménez, and the friend who was set on conquering the third Machuca sister had just arrived.

Saldaña opened a door on the hallway that led to another room, and the newly arrived guests left their coats within.

Doña Bartolita happened to enter the salon while the habanera was being played. Since no one welcomed her (because no one knew her), she hunted for a chair just like anyone else, and sat down. She was greatly relieved, as it would have been awkward to have greeted so many people. In the same way, both the Colonel and Matilde slipped into the salon, each taking a seat wherever it seemed best.

The notary came out from the coatroom with his wife, who was elegantly dressed in a white brocade dress and a silk mantilla trimmed with Prince Albert roses.

Soon a buzz could be heard from the vestibule that announced the arrival of the Machucas.

Then Saldaña approached the Colonel and whispered in his ear:

"There she is—Camacho's mistress!"

"Which one?"

"You can see her as she walks in. She's dressed in a pink gown and has feathers and flowers in her gold-dusted hair."

"Good heavens! Is that her?" the Colonel asked, coming to a halt in his tight patent-leather boots.

"That's her!" answered Saldaña with satisfaction.

Camacho's mistress crossed the floor of the salon, drawing the attention of all the guests. Without noticing that she hadn't been presented, she sat down, opened her fan, and didn't as much look at the other guests as allowed them to look upon her.

The Machucas came next. They went over to Matilde and kissed her, then greeted several of the seated women.

Directly behind the Machucas, a wave began to swell among the dandies, as though in the wake of a shark, and many entered the salon.

"Who are those young ladies?" one of the women said.

"They're the Machucas."

"I knew it had to be them."

"How did you guess?"

"I don't know; but since everyone talks about them so much . . ."

"Well, as you can see, there's nothing special about them."

"So much mascara."

"So much white powder."

"And so pretentious," added another lady.

The girls who went to the Pane Baths, their mother, and their three admirers were the next to arrive, and they found no place to sit in the salon. They stayed in the bedroom for quite a while, but no one greeted them or invited them to remove their coats. Finally, Saldaña, who was in the midst of everything, happened to pass by.

"Ladies, let me have your coats. Let's see if we can find some corner where you can find them later."

Isaura displayed her green dress in all its splendor, and Natalia showed off her jacket, the one that was made from a skirt.

There were several ladies who, finding no empty chairs in the salon, had come into the bedroom to sit on the beds and wherever else they could. The mother of Isaura, Rebeca, and Natalia did likewise, even though it was hardly amusing to stay in the bedroom. She had come to the ball to watch others dance since she was no longer able to do so herself; but with such a large crowd, she considered herself lucky to find a trunk to sit on.

Two women came into the bedroom with a rather secretive air, and every now and then they whispered to each other.

"I know what I'm talking about, I recognize him."

"But that's impossible! Such a decent young boy, and from such a good family! . . ."

"Well, don't doubt it. Ask Marianita if you want proof."

"As long as you say it's true."

"Believe me! Above all else, we must find a safe place for our coats."

"But how! Look at the state these coats are in! They're all mixed together. It will take a lot of work to find ours."

"We have no choice. Come on."

"Excuse me, excuse me," they both said as they made their way through the crowded bedroom. When they reached the corner, they began to search for their coats. No sooner had they started their operation than an inquisitive man approached them.

"What! Leaving so soon?"

"No, sir," one of the women replied.

"I mean, it would be a shame."

"We're looking for our coats in order to put them aside, that's all."

"What do they look like? I'll help."

"They're white," the other woman said while searching through the mess.

They pulled out all the white coats by their sleeves, creating even more of a jumble as they went along.

"What's this!" another interloper said. "It seems as if some of the ladies wish to leave."

"Who's leaving?"

"No one! No one is leaving!"

"What? Someone is leaving? Well then—let the party begin . . . !"

"Ah, yes!" said another bystander. He had just finished dancing and was wiping the sweat from his forehead.

In the meantime the two ladies found their coats and were carrying them on their arms while looking for someone to give them to.

"Wouldn't it be best to speak to Saldaña?" suggested the solicitous man who helped them at the beginning.

"Who is Saldaña?" one of the women asked.

"Saldaña is . . . well, he's the one who . . . he's in charge of the ball."

The women gave each other a quizzical look.

"We want to give our coats to a member of the household."

"Well, that would be Saldaña, because the family . . . the truth is, I don't know who they are."

"Well, let's give them to Saldaña, then."

"I'll call him."

After a long wait, a fatigued Saldaña appeared.

"Ladies, how can I help you?"

"We want to turn our coats over to you personally."

"Oh! But they're perfectly fine right here!"

"Nonetheless, if you would, at your convenience, be so kind as to put them in some other place . . ."

"Ah, now I understand!" Saldaña said. "So you can find them at the right moment."

"Exactly."

"What are you talking about?" asked a gentleman friend of the women who were trying to move their coats out of danger.

"For heaven's sake! What else could we be talking about than rescuing our evening coats! They've only just arrived from Paris."

"And you think there's some danger?"

"Oh, yes! Did you see who came in? . . ."

And she whispered a name into the gentleman's ear.

"Really?" he exclaimed in astonishment.

"What! You mean you don't know his trademark?"

"No, what's that?"

With the fingers of her right hand she made the universally known gesture for "thief."

"What are you saying? Oh! But he's so young, and has such a fine appearance!"

"And he's from such a good family!" the other woman added. "But it's the truth; and there's not a single ball he's attended where coats weren't lost."

"Are you sure it's him?" the gentleman insisted, still doubtful.

"Yes, sir, he's the one! He's been caught *in flagrante*, and on one occasion a lost coat was retrieved in a pawnshop he had taken it to."

"Well, if you say it's true. . . . But it doesn't seem possible! In any event, what were you doing?"

"We gave our coats to . . . what's his name?"

"Saldaña," her friend answered.

"That's it! To a Señor Saldaña who is the . . ."

"Yes, I already know Saldaña! Oh yes, Saldaña! In that case, don't worry. He put them away for you?"

"Yes, he did, personally, and he assured us that they would be safe."

While this scene was taking place in a corner of one of the bedrooms, Saldaña went back and forth from the dining room to the salon, from the salon to the kitchen, and from the kitchen to the bedrooms. In the salon, he was the master of ceremonies; in the dining room, the steward; in the kitchen, the majordomo; and in the bedrooms, the coat checker.

Everyone was searching for Saldaña; everyone asked for him; and he was all over, flushed with heat, sweat, and exhaustion, but as solicitous and indefatigable as ever.

While a polka was playing, the fashionable young men from the Pane Baths and the Plaza de Iturbide (along with the coat thief) slipped into the dining room. The most intrepid of them took a corkscrew out of his pocket and opened a bottle of cognac. Saldaña's special cognac! They discovered his Santa Barbara; they smelled it out of its hiding place. When he appeared again in the dining room, they said:

"Señor Saldaña, come have a glass of cognac with us."

"Yes, let's drink to the health of Señor Saldaña!"

"It's excellent! We can tell it was you who bought the liquor."

"Let's have some more!"

"Where's Federico?"

"So the cognac meets with your approval . . . ?" Saldaña said without managing to disguise his anger.

"Oh, it's excellent!" another young man said while drinking his second glass.

"Eat something, or else it'll go to your head," another young man told him. "Take this sandwich."

"Is that a ham sandwich?"

"Yes. Do you want another?"

"No."

The Santa Barbara passed through the everyone's hands except Saldaña's, who was being praised to the heavens. Meanwhile, he stewed in a soup of his own making.

The avalanche could no longer be held back. The cognac's bouquet reached into the salon and beckoned to its devotees, who constituted a majority of the guests.

The young man with the corkscrew, proud of his foresight and ingenuity, kept offering drinks to friends and strangers.

"You see," he told his friend, "before I come to these events, the first thing I do is slip a corkscrew into my pocket."

"Well done."

"Do you want some sherry?"

"No, I'd prefer a cognac."

"Good choice. It's first class."

"Listen, my friend," another young man said to Federico, "let's save a bottle of this cognac."

"Why do you want it?"

"I offered it to Patrocinio."

"Let's offer it together. Go ahead, take one."

"Let me through, then."

He squeezed through the crowd until he was within an arm's length of the cognac. The minute everyone's back was turned, he stuffed a bottle into the inner pocket of his frock coat.

"Gentlemen, please." Saldaña could barely be heard. He realized that the locusts were in full possession of everything that was edible. "The ladies need something to eat."

"Good, I'll take care of it," said a young man who was gulping down a slice of cake.

In spiteful indignation, and with a carelessness born of fatigue, Saldaña upended an entire basket of pastries onto a large tray. As might be guessed, they fell into a pitiful disarray.

And what would have happened if those young chickens, who were so used to kernels of corn showering down on them every which way, had felt some aesthetic scruples and turned those pastries right side up!

One young man stepped forward to offer the pastries to the ladies, while several others arranged the pièce de résistance on another large tray that took two of them to carry. It held dozens of glasses in all different sizes, which were being filled with sweet wine, anisette, and, above all, cognac.

"Don't pour so much cognac. These drinks are for the ladies."

"But they all drink cognac, my friend. You'll see."

"Don't say such things."

"Just wait; you'll see how few of them choose wine."

Followed by two other youths carrying bottles ("for refreshments," they said), the cupbearers made their rounds, led by Saldaña, who cleared a path through the multitudes assembled in the bedrooms.

With great difficulty, they carried the trays around the salon, weaving in and out between the dancers and the ladies who remained seated, and barely avoiding a mishap on more than one occasion. If the drinks managed to escape misfortune, however, the same could not be said of the pastries. At the very moment a dandy raised his arm to gulp down a cream puff, an out-of-control waltzer, who was steering Camacho's mistress on a dizzying course, bumped his shoulder into the dandy's elbow, and the pastry went flying onto the blue dress worn by the mother of Saldaña's little ones.

When Lupe felt this missile land, she let out an involuntary scream and jumped to her feet, attempting to free herself; but it was too late. The pastry slid down her dress and landed on the carpet, where the cream spread out in full.

"Someone's going to fall on that."

"Did your dress get stained, miss?" one of the dancers asked Lupe.

"Look," she replied, pointing to a yellow streak dribbling down the length of her dress.

"Here's a handkerchief."

Another woman took the handkerchief and cleaned Lupe's dress. Meanwhile, Saldaña, who had an eye on everything, ran to the kitchen, shouting:

"Attention! I need someone to clean the carpet!"

"You go, Doña Pachita," said one of the servants who had served herself a double ration of the anisette. "You go, 'cause you work here, an' we're only for the night."

Francisca entered the salon with a wet cloth in hand. As a sign of respect, she covered her head with her rebozo.

Although when compared to most in her guild, she was a bit more refined and not as dirty, Francisca could be called, rightly or wrongly, "a garbanzo." She was dressed in the traditional floor-length cotton skirt, a tunic cut from the same fabric, and the national rebozo.

The families of the conquistadors who came to live in the Indies preferred to have as their servants those Indians who had already started to mumble some words of Spanish; and although in the beginning these servants continued to eat corn and chili peppers, little by little they yielded to Spanish tastes, which other Indians considered a breach of trust and a treasonous crime.

One of the foods introduced by the Spaniards was the garbanzo bean, a legume that no Spanish pot has gone without since the days of El Cid. This bean, which was one of many items intended for the conquistador's comfort, was imported from the mother country for many years despite its easy acclimation and cultivation in Mexico. It so happened that the Indian, besides stumbling over the language of the white man, began to eat the garbanzos of his master, and was consequently known as a "garbancero," or bean-eater, as a sign of patriotic disrespect. This nickname, which has been handed down for three centuries, has become solidified through use; and in the case of the young female servant it has a malicious double meaning. If the Royal Academy of the Spanish Language adopted the expressions of its former colonies, if only to enlighten those who read stories about our way of life, it would add to its entry for "garbanzo" these two definitions:

GARBANCERO [fr. Mex]: male domestic servant of the indigenous or mestizo class who speaks Spanish and eats garbanzo beans.

GARBANZO: young female servant having the same characteristics as the garbancero.

We do not need to point out or explain the ideological link that exists between the "garbanzo" and the young man of fashion, for these analogies belong to the private realm; however, as your faithful narrator, we cannot fail to report that Francisca wasn't able to pass through the pantry, not to mention the hallway, without being fondly patted and pinched. (A proverbial episode in the chronicles of kitchens and balls such as the one being given by Saldaña.)

"How was't, Doña Pachita?" the talkative pot scrubber asked her.

"How d'you think?" Francisca replied angrily.

"What'd you clean?"

"Somethin' like *atole** that's in those pastries."

"Like an egg?"

"Yea, and thick."

"That's called crim," the cook said.

"I'll never go in there," said the servant who smelled of anisette. "If you're poor, keep to the kitchen."

"Damn them rich devils!" Francisca exclaimed.

"Wha'd they do, Doña Pachita?"

"You can't go anywhere without 'em pinching you," Francisca answered, rubbing her left forearm.

"You see, Doña Pachita? I'd never . . . Just 'cause we're servants . . ."

"Well now I know! It's one thing t' be poor, but it's another thing t' be—"

---

* A drink made from ground corn.

How the Heat from Candles,
Combined with a Santa Barbara
Cognac and Other Evils,
Can Create Pandemonium at a Ball

From the moment the first young men flocked into the dining room, the guests descended upon the pastries with the voraciousness of locusts. This insect from the acrididae family swoops down on all that is green and makes it vanish: such is its destructive mission. The guests who invaded Saldaña's *sancta sanctorum* appeared to be on a similar mission to devour everything made from grain and all that was liquid.

There were a few people standing in the doorway who were amused by this scene of devastation. They noticed that many youths had installed themselves in the dining room for hours, oblivious to what was happening in the salon, as their sole intent was to eat and drink.

Saldaña had no other defense against this war of extermination than to withdraw food from the storehouse and distribute rations.

"What are you doing, Saldaña?" Bartolita's husband asked.

"Colonel, what else can I do? Here I am with some friends, about to embark on a veritable crusade to ward off the invasion. Six of us are in charge of removing the food from the table and distributing it throughout the salon, the hallways, and wherever else guests may be."

"What ill-mannered young men!" one lady said to another.

"It mustn't be tolerated. The reason I didn't want to bring my daughters was that I suspected a gang of them would be here, helping themselves to the liquor and getting drunk."

"And there's more to come! May the Lord deliver us!"

"What do you mean?"

"Up to now they seem to be in their senses; but give them another half an hour, and there'll be no order left."

"Just listen to them shout! They're becoming too excited; I think we'd better leave."

"First, I'd like a glass of water."

"Me, too."

"Would you care for something?" a man who was getting on in years asked them. He was, to be exact, the notary, who because of a vestige of . . . a vestige of love, didn't want to see his wife dancing with someone else, and so, against his own scruples, had taken refuge in the dining room.

"We'd like some water."

"Would you like some wine?"

"Thank you, sir, but no."

"Some pastries . . . sweets . . ."

"Just water, if you wouldn't mind."

The notary looked for water in that den of iniquity, and after a futile search, had to enter the kitchen.

"Some water, if you please," he said, sticking his head inside the door.

"Drinking water?" the talkative servant asked.

"Yes, for two ladies."

"Wha' does the gen'l'man want?" the cook asked.

"He's lookin' for water," another servant said.

"Here's the water," the pot scrubber said, wrapping her rebozo around her face with one hand while extending a pitcher to the notary with the other.

The notary drew back when he saw this chipped and blackened pitcher.

"It's fresh from the barrel," she protested. She veiled her mouth again with the rebozo.

"Yes, but . . . isn't there a carafe or pitcher that's more presentable?"

"No sir, nothin' that belongs to this house," Francisca replied, "just among the rented things, an' only Don Saldaña knows about that."

The notary had to choose between letting the ladies die of thirst or bringing them the pitcher. He opted for the latter, and when he returned to the dining room he looked for a glass.

"What are you doing with that pitcher, sir?" one of the young men asked.

"It's pulque," another one added.

"No, it's water," the notary answered, irritated.

He went up to the thirsty ladies. "You must forgive me, but I couldn't find anything except this pitcher to hold the water."

"You went to so much trouble for us," one of the ladies said.

"It was no trouble at all," he replied.

The ladies drank the water that came out of the ugly, grimy pitcher while looking at each other.

"Hey!" one of the young dandies said. "Look at the pitchers they're using."

"Who's got a pitcher?" his friend asked.

"Look over there!"

"What about it?"

"Nothing, it's a pitcher, like all the rest."

People started talking about the pitcher so much that the notary placed it under the table as soon after he poured a second glass.

Meanwhile, Enrique had been formally presented to Leonor, and both he and Jiménez had been promised several dances. On their own, the guests had divided themselves into different groups, as though each had found the place that corresponded to his station. The dancers assembled in the salon; they, of course, cared little for libations, which is a mark in their favor, and which also proves that an education in manners keeps young people away from vices and bad habits.

Indeed, as a complement to one's education, dancing is an indispensable branch of learning in all cultured societies. Young people who have never attended dancing school secretly possess a withdrawn, unpleasant disposition that makes them solitary and disagreeable. Those who can dance, however, have managed to cut the gordian knot of achieving a sound education in morals, which has no small influence on an individual's future.

Let us take, for example, two opposite types from the present scene (the one closest to hand) and examine them.

Jiménez was a dancer. Perico, one of the dandies who played billiards at the Plaza de Iturbide, was not.

Jiménez did not drink. Perico went out carousing every night.

The gordian knot we referred to is this: Jiménez discovered, while dancing, that a young man and woman can enjoy a pure and innocent pleasure, and that swaying with a partner in time to the beat can be a legitimate pastime, one that is entirely inoffensive and not in the least transcendental. Furthermore, however far evil and depravity can go in these matters, there is a line at which a man is able to stop, quite effortlessly, despite the vehemence of his passions. And finally, it is through dancing that a certain wicked spirit is banished that only serves to send young lovers down a dark, torturous path.

Perico was just the opposite. Because of his education, he had been kept away from the fair sex, and with no mother or sisters, he only knew the life of a schoolboy. The first woman he had any contact with was a servant, and he fell in love with her. For Perico there could be no contact between the two sexes that wasn't love, or for the sake of love: a sincere, innocent encounter seemed illusory; he didn't understand that a man could approach a woman for reasons that were unrelated to love. Perico, as audacious as he appeared, trembled before young girls; he was almost frightened of them. Then his virile instincts rebelled, and he took revenge on his own weakness by falling in love with the first woman he met. As we said, Perico couldn't dance; but after a few drinks went to his head, he would enter a salon like a wolf and choose his victim: these sheep served no other purpose than to be devoured.

Perico was among those who had been in the dining room ever since the ball began, smoking with his friends and having one drink after another. He entered into a state of excitement that, on account of his shyness, he had deliberately sought; and he started to feel a certain brio and energy, a certain resolve, to stand face-to-face with a young girl. It was only by these means that he dared to set foot in the salon, and although he became lost in the crowd, we can follow all his actions. He stopped in the middle of the room, put his hands behind his back, and with an arrogant gaze surveyed the feminine forms on the dance floor, as if he were in a slaughterhouse measuring the dimensions of a cow. He was selecting his partner.

Let us leave him in that pose while we turn to some of our other characters.

Enrique had at last succeeded in offering his arm to Leonor for a waltz. It was practically their only opportunity to talk to each other with ease.

And how beautiful she looked! She and Enrique were so closely matched in height that when they spoke, their words flowed back and forth along the same horizontal line, which made conversation pleasant and smooth.

Leonor had, moreover, a peculiar way of taking her partner's arm. She leaned quite a bit forward and at an oblique angle to her companion in order to catch his words more exactly. This forward inclination, besides favoring her protruding curves, placed her body in contact with Enrique's arm, and was one of her characteristic gestures.

Enrique was thrown into a state of confusion. The first thing he did was fill his lungs with a cubic foot of the hot air in the salon, which was permeated by the Corilopsis perfume arising from Leonor's lacy bosom.

It was enough to make his mouth water.

And Leonor's eyes, when seen up close, had a unique charm of their own. Their appearance changed completely: they had a somewhat savage, unruly nature that resisted all attempts at refinement. Leonor's indomitable look had a certain wild ferocity;

and her thick, slightly curled, black eyelashes gave her a commanding air that could not be concealed. Leonor owed her great popularity to her singular gaze, and perhaps this was what had subjugated Enrique.

As we mentioned earlier, the Machucas danced well, and as they had slim waists and agile limbs, they would waltz with a young man in dizzying turns, until he was overcome by his good fortune and their voluptuosity.

Enrique set forth on this flight, and grabbed hold of Leonor with the first tremor of his passion, behaving in much the same way as a mad butterfly when it hooks its tiny legs onto the petals of a just-opened bloom that is rough with pollen, moist with dew, and rich with fragrance.

There he waltzed, hypnotized by the lights circling round his head, his words in harmony with the notes of the flute, his respiration in time with the chords of the double bass. As he exhaled, his breath mingled with the chemical effluvia of her perfume and with the hot air filtered through her bronchi. And then and there he declared his love, all his love, using those broken phrases that leap out before we know it, assuming an eloquence that no madrigal or idyll can ever match.

Without a moment's thought, Leonor let herself be swept away: she entered Enrique's magnetic circle, and fixed her big dark eyes on him like a fox holding its easy prey. Enrique could feel an electric tingling in his left hand, which he placed on Leonor's satin waistband; and after taking control of the nerve endings in her left hand, he felt as if an inevitable fusion between two organisms had taken place, or as if a fiery blowtorch had melted two metals into a single liquid.

All of a sudden, the music stopped. Enrique was like a thirsty man whose glass was snatched away from his lips.

"Play on!" someone shouted.

"Play on!!" other voices chimed in.

And the music resumed.

The guests formed a circle around the two couples who were dancing, as some enthusiasts said, "divinely."

The two couples dancing the waltz were Enrique and Leonor, who were dancing exceptionally well, and Perico and Gumesinda.

How was it possible that Perico, who couldn't dance, drew so much attention that a circle formed around him?

Enrique was perhaps the only man there who knew how to dance; Perico had never waltzed before in his life. Enrique understood the aesthetics of dancing, and without being effeminate, moved gracefully, with a natural expression and an agreeable physiognomy. In every respect, one could tell he was a gentleman from high society who had been taught how to dance.

As we saw earlier, Perico had come into the salon to choose a partner. He found Gumesinda to his liking, and asked her for the next habanera.

"I've already promised them all," Gumesinda replied. "Can you dance the waltz?"

And Perico, with the recklessness of ignorance, said yes; and in an act of audacity that only the cognac could have induced, took Gumesinda out for a spin. It so happened, however, that by following the rhythm (and Gumesinda's lead), he was able to catch on to the steps, or rather, to guess what they were, like someone who learns how to swim by throwing himself into the water.

Perico, swelled by his burst of folly, believed for a moment that he was the king of the ball. He was happy; but his happiness, which was of a different order from Enrique's, began to reach troublesome proportions. After the first few turns, he began to lose track of his surroundings. Black and yellow lines crossed his field of vision with a dizzying speed; murmurs and a crashing din, as from a choir and a waterfall at the same time, distorted the music in the same way that colors, when oscillated, become distorted. Who knows how he managed to hold onto Gumesinda! What kind of posture, balance, and skill kept him attached? But Perico, who was swept into the concentric circles of a whirlpool, began to lose consciousness. Suddenly, as if he had reached the outermost circle, or like a stone from a slingshot that flies off into space, Perico felt a jolt, an explosion, a flash of light, and then everything became silent, dark, and still.

He lay sprawled on the carpet with his arms spread out, as if dead! . . . Gumesinda shrieked and raised her arms, and a wave of guests surged forward and cried:

"What happened?"

Machuca, the paymaster, had launched an enormous stone at poor Perico, leaving him prostrate on the floor.

"What happened? What is it?" many voices exclaimed.

"Nothing! An accident!"

"He's been hit!"

"He was punched in the face!"

"Someone's hurt!!"

"Someone's been killed!!!"

The news reached the kitchen: "Someone's been killed!"

"Ave Maria!" the cook exclaimed. "Now those devils are throwin' punches."

"Wha'd we do now, Doña Pachita?"

"Who was killed?"

"They say his name's Perico."

"And who was it that hit 'em?"

"Someone called Machuca."

"With a gun?"

"Prob'ly a knife," one of the servants said.

"And he's dead, then?"

"I'll take a look."

In the meantime, the ladies had rushed into the hall. It took four men to pick Perico up and carry him into the bedroom.

The guests thought they saw blood when it was nothing more than cognac. People continued to shout: "Someone's been killed!" "How awful!" "Let's go!"

"Girls, get our coats!"

"Let's get out of here! Forget about the coats."

"Lola, where are you?"

"Where are my daughters? Blessed Virgin!"

Like oil from water, the women separated from the men, who remained standing around the body.

"It was nothing. Only a stone."

"What a shot!"

"Machuca is strong."

"Listen, everyone, there's no reason for alarm. Perico isn't even knocked out. Doctor, have a look," someone said to Capetillo, who was one of the guests.

Capetillo examined Perico, and made his sole diagnosis by

straightening the pinkie and thumb of his right hand while folding down his other three fingers, a well-known sign for drunkenness, which greatly amused the bystanders.

Indeed, Perico had suffered no wounds, but the cognac, the waltz, and the stone were enough to keep him out of combat.

"It's nothing, gentlemen, nothing at all. If you would please calm down and take your seats. Come, gentlemen. Let's dance!"

"Yes, let the bodies fall where they may, what does it matter!" one of the dandies exclaimed.

"There's one down, now let's dance."

"How about an habanera!"

"Order! Order!"

But nothing could stem the agitation and alarm that had spread among the ladies.

The stone-throwing Machuca had vanished on the spot, out of prudence or shame over what he had done.

Saldaña, Doña Bartolita, and her husband managed to stop several women who were coming down the stairs, and urged them to return to the salon. The room with the coats was in a state of utmost confusion and disorder. Hats had been flattened and coats trampled, and there were great piles of woolen and silk coats whose tassels, fringes, and embroidery had become knotted together, making it impossible to separate them.

"What are you doing?" one young lady said to another.

"Look at this mess! Here's my coat, but it's so tangled with these other two that I can't get it out. I've already torn several fringes, but it still won't come. It's as if all three coats were woven together."

"Pull here."

"Oops, it's ripping! Whose coat is that?"

"It doesn't matter, just pull, because we're leaving."

Although Saldaña, the notary, Don Manuel and several guests had been able to contain the commotion in the halls and bedrooms, the dining room was like Agramant's camp.* The young

* Agramant was the Muslim general who laid siege to Paris in *Orlando Furioso*. His camp was the scene of disorder and chaos (described in canto 27 of the poem).

men began to debate whether Machuca was justified or not in his actions. There were those who affirmed that Perico had kissed Gumesinda, others who claimed he was holding her in an unseemly manner, and still others who said he was making a vulgar declaration of love. The fact is, they all became quite agitated, some in favor, and others against, Machuca.

Music filled the salon once more. Meanwhile, two drunken guests were exchanging heated words, and a bottle of red wine went flying through the air, striking the glass front of a cabinet with an infernal crash that was followed by shouts and more tumult.

"Gentleman, stop! Calm down!" Saldaña exclaimed. His hair was in disarray, and his collar was drenched in sweat and as loose as a chicken's dewlap. "Calm down!"

No sooner had he uttered those words than there was a gun blast, more shouts, and the whistle of a gendarme.

"All hell's broken loose!" Saldaña exclaimed, leaping down the steps four at a time. "What's going on?"

"There are gunshots in the street!" voices yelled from the hall.

"Another fight!"

"They must have been drinking!"

A crowd of people rushed down the stairs behind Saldaña. Outside, the gendarmes were shining their lanterns in all directions, and the alarm spread by their whistles could be heard for ten square blocks.

"Let's see! What happened?"

"Who fired the gun?" a gendarme asked.

"Who's been shot?" shouted another.

"Who's been wounded?"

The Colonel, despite his tight boots, was out in the street and, having taken off his hat, was ready for combat.

"What happened?"

"Machuca and Pío Cenizo are throwing punches."

"Why?"

"Because of Perico."

And indeed, Cenizo and Machuca had been pulled apart and were both in the hands of the gendarmes.

The Colonel asserted his authority, and severely reprimanded the officers. He attempted to have Machuca and Cenizo freed, claiming that they were gentlemen and who knows what else.

The gendarmes, who touched their fingers to their kepis and stood at attention, asserted that they were carrying out their duties. The Colonel, greatly irritated by their answer, proclaimed that he was a real man who had spilled blood for his country, and that moreover . . . and believing that the words he was about to say would disarm them so completely that they would bury the matter, he placed his hand on an officer's shoulder and said in an emphatic undertone:

"Porfirio Díaz . . . is a close friend of mine . . ."

The gendarme was unmoved.

Once again the Colonel whispered into the gendarme's ear:

"Carlos Díez Gutiérrez* is my daughter's godfather."

The gendarme didn't respond. Despite the cabalistic nature of those formidable declarations, two compact circles of gendarmes, in whose midst were Cenizo and Machuca, headed toward Police Headquarters.

The shattering of glass in the dining room, the altercation between the two men, the shouts and whistles outside, and the moans and cries of the ladies, all combined to create a scene of utter chaos and confusion in the Colonel's house.

Groups of ladies rushed down the stairs to find a safe exit, while others came inside the doorway and raced up the stairs to spread the alarm. The room with the coats had become a veritable pigsty, as no one bothered to look where they were stepping. One young man walked over the hats and frock coats just for fun.

The group in the street, with the help of an obliging official, fortunately found a way to keep the police from hauling off the two contenders. Meanwhile, all the families who wished to leave squeezed madly through the door.

Poor Saldaña caught his second wind, and had the musicians resume playing in order to drown out the wild cries and even the obscene words of the drunken young men.

---

* Secretary of the Government for a brief period during the presidency of Porfirio Díaz.

More than three-quarters of the guests had disappeared; but one veteran had stayed behind, testifying to her valor and sense of civic duty.

Venturita had stayed behind. How could she leave? The gentleman who wanted to see her feet, the one for whom Venturita had taken a long, formal walk one Sunday from the Zócalo to the Hotel de Iturbide, whose reticence and apparent indifference led Venturita to ponder the aesthetics of the shoe—this same gentleman was at the ball, and he had approached Venturita, danced with her, and told her many gallant things. And at the end, when Venturita ran to the bedroom like Ione on the last day of Pompeii in order to save herself from the catastrophe, this gentleman said with a dramatic flourish: "Don't leave."

Venturita raised her intelligent eyes, fixed them on her Glaucus, and threw her white coat on the ruins in the bedroom.

How could Venturita leave!

Other veterans who survived the catastrophe were the Machuca sisters. Each could be found tête-à-tête with a young man: Leonor with Enrique, Gumesinda with Jiménez, and the youngest sister with Jiménez's friend.

Lupe, in her blue cream-stained dress, could no longer keep her eyes open despite the fun she had had. She looked for a corner where she could rest her head without being seen. No one had fallen in love with Lupe. She was ugly, the poor thing, and badly shaped, and then there were those defiant bangs that feigned docility when wet, but as soon as the temperature in the salon climbed, began to rebel with a ferocious tenacity. Her forehead was covered not by curls that fall and shade the eye, but rather, by black bristles that stood straight up as if they were holding a grudge against a pair of scissors.

With such bangs, it is quite understandable why her escort, Don Lucio the barber, was the only one who danced with her.

It was almost three in the morning, and the poor Colonel still couldn't put on his old boots. He was completely lame, and avoided moving from his chair at all costs.

Matilde danced a great deal and was hardly alarmed. Doña Bartolita was suffering from frightful gas, her clothes felt tight, and she wanted it all to end soon.

The candle in the kitchen had gone out and the servants, induced by the darkness, fell asleep. Because the anisette had been followed by cognac and champagne and great quantities of pastries, cheese, and cold cuts, they had a very refreshing and comfortable sleep, at least from all appearances.

Camacho's mistress had been among the first to disappear without saying good-bye. Enriqueta and Don Manuel followed her lead.

The two ladies who had given their coats to Saldaña for safekeeping were searching for him all over in order to reclaim their coats and leave. Since Saldaña was at the center of everything, he heard his name being called and, anticipating the ladies' request, he looked for the coats in their hiding place.

"Damn!" he exclaimed, clenching his teeth and opening his eyes wide. The closet had been sacked; its wooden boards flaunted their nakedness. Saldaña was well acquainted with the chaos that had reigned; from past experience, he knew there were always coat thieves at balls like this one. Even though he was responsible, he didn't want to be blamed by the women who had been cleaned out of their possessions. He ran into the kitchen and, stumbling past the sleeping servants, crossed the darkness to hide in a small patio.

The outcry for Saldaña echoed throughout the house, but by eight o'clock that evening he had already grown tired of hearing his name called, and stopped answering.

The ladies searched for their hostess, and it was then that they finally met Bartolita.

They presented their complaints with the greatest decorum.

"Saldaña! Where is Saldaña?"

The Colonel and various assistants swept through the house; but Saldaña couldn't be found, and some claimed that he had left. The ladies looked for their coats in the closet and, like Saldaña, discovered it was empty.

Doña Bartolita had to offer them something to wear home, and she promised to send them their coats when they were found.

Immediately behind the ladies were two gentlemen who had lost their frock coats. As far as the hats were concerned, the only ones that remained were old and several were crushed.

Saldaña was in the patio listening to the tempest roar, and decided to keep his nose out of sight.

Lupe and Don Lucio were among those searching for him. They had already decided to leave without him when they passed by a room whose window opened out onto the patio. A cautious voice emerged from the crack.

"Lucio, come here."

"What? Who is it? Is that you?"

"Yes."

"Saldaña?"

"Shh! Be quiet! Turn your back and pretend no one's here. Now, listen."

"All right."

"Be careful."

"Yes."

"Get your hat and take Lupe with you."

"Yes."

"Shh! . . . Listen."

"What?"

"When you go down the stairs . . ."

"Yes, what . . . ?"

"Stop at the bottom. On your right, in the barrel behind the eucalyptus tree, you'll find a basket."

"And?"

"It's nothing, I just put some leftovers aside for my boys."

"Understood. Good night."

Lupe could do nothing else but put her fingers through the window crack. On the other side, Saldaña quietly bit them.

Lupe and Don Lucio left.

Saldaña decided not to leave his hiding place as long as he was being called. For a long time he heard his name repeated in a full range of tones, but he didn't move. This short respite, after hustling and bustling for so many hours, induced him to sit down. The patio in which he found himself was jammed with empty crates and packing straw. By searching with his hands, Saldaña was quickly able to find a crate that could be turned into a seat.

As he bent his legs, it occurred to him that he hadn't sat down since late afternoon.

The darkest hours reigned. As the echoes from the ball gradually faded, other sounds could be heard in the kitchen and the patio.

The pot scrubbers were snoring, if not with the happiness of the righteous, then at least with the slumbers brought on by the anisette and the satisfactions of an exotic dinner.

A few snored in rhythm; others grunted; still others wheezed; all together, between their raucous breathing and the crackle of the straw, they sounded like a chorus of frogs. They were in the land of dreams, the kingdom of Morpheus. Saldaña added his own stupendous yawn to this chorus, a yawn that followed forty-eight hours of duty, and before he realized that his name was no longer being called, he fell fast asleep!

The ball ended of its own accord: little by little, the guests left without saying good-bye.

Bartolita went to bed, and Matilde and her papa put out the candles.

I X

Conclusion

S oon after, the sun rose. Dawn arrived with its clean, blue-tinged rays, revealing a scene of debauchery that had only recently been abandoned by human swine.

Out of the dining room and the salon came a vapor reeking of alcohol and human smells, so heavy that it practically crawled along the floor, as if reluctant to do battle with the pure, diaphanous atmosphere of the morning. A rose-colored light peeked through the balustrade on the balcony and spied on the ruins in the dining room, which looked like Agramant's camp. The light filtered through the curtains and crept between the flower pots, painting blue fillets on the wine glasses and the candelabras, whose candles had dripped a trail of stearine wax onto the tablecloths. The carpet was drenched in wine and planted with shards of broken glass; there was Gruyère cheese on the chairs, under the tables, inside the glasses and on hats; and squashed pastries covered whatever flowers were still visible in the carpet. The table exhibited all the scars of battle, as more bottles and glasses were broken and overturned than were left standing.

The Gruyère cheese spread a path into the salon; it was smeared on picture frames and chairs, on candelabras, plaster columns, and spittoons, and was ground into the floor. There wasn't a single flat surface that wasn't covered by a half-empty glass, a pastry, or a piece of cheese. The guests had been given more than they wanted and more than they could have ever consumed, and at some point they realized they were holding far too much.

While the guests, now at home, spread gossip about the ball (from which we shall spare our good readers), let us listen to the impressions of Enrique, the ardent admirer of Leonor Machuca.

As it was Sunday afternoon, he followed his usual habit and went on a walk. It wasn't long before he met up with his friend and Jiménez.

"How are you, Enrique? Did you stay up all night?" Jiménez asked him.

"I couldn't keep my eyes closed. I haven't slept since yesterday."

"That's a good sign. Something big must have happened."

"Oh! Now it's clear—your triumph is complete," added Enrique's friend.

"Tell us, Enrique, about your impressions."

"As long as we sit . . . over there," he said, gesturing toward the Alameda, "on a secluded bench."

"Splendid! That way we can hear each other."

"Let's go."

And the three friends settled down on a bench in the most deserted section of the park.

"Well, gentlemen," Enrique exclaimed, lifting his hand to his forehead and squinting his eyes as if to concentrate on his ideas. "I've been saved!"

"How?"

"Listen closely. When I was introduced to Leonor, we shook hands and . . . it was a question of magnetism . . . I went off the deep end. When her hand squeezed mine, my resolve was suddenly strengthened, and with the arrogance of a man who has burned all his bridges, I got down to business, and spoke to Leonor for the first time. I asked her some questions and . . . you're not going to believe this, but that woman's voice had the strangest effect on me. I couldn't believe such a voice could come from that body; I felt I had mistaken someone else for her. That is, the impression her figure made didn't agree at all with the impression made by her voice. But it wasn't simply a matter of acoustics; the moral and intellectual content of her answers was disappointing as well. Leonor, despite her elegance, is completely vulgar, in every sense of the word. What do you think is the only topic of conversation that excited her?"

"Love," Jiménez and his friend said in unison.

"No sir, that would have been only natural. It wasn't love; it was gambling."

"Gambling!"

"Yes! Leonor is a gambler, and plays for high stakes. She told me, with a bravado worthy of Martel,* that three days ago she hit the jackpot, and then immediately lost the fifty pesos that she wagered for a stranger who had fallen in love with her. With a scandalous naïveté, this woman bragged about her attempts to ruin this suitor by playing the odds. I confess it had a detestable effect on me; but what completely put an end to my illusions was something else."

"What was that?" Jiménez and his friend asked with great interest.

"Leonor is a drunk."

"It can't be."

"My word of honor. I stopped dancing with her, and from the hall I could watch her as she was getting something to eat. She took off the gloves that shaped her hands and concealed her complexion, and a bony, dark, coarse hand stretched out to devour pastries and drinks.

"When I saw her again in the salon, those big eyes that had so enchanted me now had the vague and stupid look of intoxication, and her eyelids were streaked red. It was she who spoke first . . . slurring her words, making needless repetitions, and then to top it all off, finally declaring:

" 'You must excuse me . . . I'm not exactly tipsy, because it never goes to my head, as he can tell you,' she said, placing her hand on another young man's shoulder, 'but look, between the three of us,

* Reference to Don Felipe Martel, a gambling impresario who operated several casinos in Mexico City.

we've had two bottles of champagne, and besides that, I've had six cognacs, but my head is still clear. The only thing is, my eyes are burning like there's smoke, that's all . . .'

"At this point Leonor let out an idiotic giggle, and I could see her body wobble involuntarily, like a drunk whose equilibrium is threatened by excessive gas.

"This sprite, the poetic creation of my fantasy, whose irresistible beauty could, with one glance, put my future and my existence at her feet—this woman has evaporated: she doesn't exist, she never existed. I am, therefore, a free man, and shall return to Europe. Thank you for inviting me to the ball, because now I know what to think about the Machucas."

"Well, I'm not as scrupulous as Enrique," Jiménez said. "Just as I said, I gave Gumesinda a few drinks, and everything worked out fine."

"And as for me," the other friend said, "the youngest sister gave me three kisses last night, and promised me three more."

Three days have passed since the ball, and Doña Bartolita's house still reeks of cognac from her doorstep. Her carpets and most of the upholstery could not withstand a second ball. The poor colonel hasn't yet finished paying the bills which, when added to the unforeseen expenses arising from the breakage and destruction, have exhausted all his funds, and plunged him into debt.

Don Lucio, following Saldaña's instructions, carried away a big basket full of bottles, tins, pastries, cheese, and whatever else was worthy of the name "leftovers." The next day, Don Lucio, Saldaña, Lupe, and the little ones ate until they burst.

The girls who visit the Pane Baths didn't go for a dip that Sunday; they were tingling with the heat of the ball, and savored it fully. They had danced a great deal with their admirers.

Finally, Doña Bartolita, overcome by exhaustion, embarrassed by the coats that were lost and the scandals that broke out in her home, irritated by the neighbors' gossip, and in distress over her husband's ruin, exclaimed with an eloquence she had never felt capable of before:

"My dear husband, that was the first and last time! We must be like everyone else, selfish. We should have known our ball would end in a brawl. Better leave the next one to the neighbors!"

CHRISTMAS EVE

NEGATIVES EXPOSED
FROM DECEMBER 24
TO DECEMBER 25, 1882

I

"Look, Lupe, there's my boyfriend!"

"Which one?"

"The one with the dark moustache."

Lupe looked him over carefully.

"What do you think?"

"He looks nice."

"The poor thing!"

"Why?"

"Just imagine, he hasn't been invited to any posadas.*"

"And you believe him?"

"Of course, my dear Lupe, since he's such a good—"

"That means you're not going to be together on Christmas Eve."

"That's right. That's why I'm so upset."

"Poor Otilia! Poor lovebirds! I'm so glad —"

"Glad about what?"

"Glad I'm not in love."

* Nightly celebrations held from December 16 through December 24 that commemorate the journey of Mary and Joseph to Bethlehem before the birth of Christ.

"You hypocrite! What about the General?"

"Shh! Be quiet."

"See what I mean?"

"All right, but that's not love. You're so bad! And all because of what I told you the other night."

"I know what I'm doing: and when I talk about the General with you . . ."

"Aren't you a bad girl!"

"Piñatas, ladies, piñatas!" shouted a peddler who came up between Lupe and Otilia.

"Who cares about piñatas," Lupe said, grumpily.

"You mean you're not going to buy one, miss?" the peddler said, tipping his hat. "You told me you wanted a bride for your Christmas Eve piñata."

"I did?"

"Yes, miss. I'm the same one who was here the other afternoon."

"Oh, yes, now I remember."

"So, we'll take't to the General's 'hoose'?"

Lupe turned red.

"Go on, you naughty girl," whispered Otilia in her ear.

"How much is it?"

"You already know, m'lady. Fourteen reales."

"Well, all right."

"I'll take't to his 'hoose,' then? I know the way."

And the peddler, with a crepe-paper bride in one hand and a general in the other, disappeared.

"And why does the Christmas Eve piñata have to be a bride?" Otilia asked Lupe.

"I can't tell you."

"You're so bad! And the other night you dared to put up a piñata of a general! What do you intend to do with the bride?"

Lupe and Otilia lowered their voices and turned down a narrow lane lined with open stalls selling Christmas decorations on the Plaza de la Constitución.* The young man with the dark moustache, who followed them at a certain distance, managed to catch Otilia's eye only a few times across a colorful display of piñatas, lanterns, and the Holy Pilgrims, Mary and Joseph.

---

* The central plaza in Mexico City, also known as the Zócalo.

II

The man selling the piñatas arrived at the General's "hoose" (as he called it), and since we are scrupulous historians, we should warn our readers about certain types of property transfers and bogus military titles. In this day and age, it is not uncommon to meet a general who isn't really a general at all; and as far as "his hoose" is concerned, we fancy there is plenty to be said on the subject.

Lupe and Otilia arrived at the house after the electric lights had been turned on.

The peddler delivered the bride and was given fourteen reales. As the coins warmed in his hand, he began to think that the General's "hoose" looked promising, and decided he shouldn't leave. So he offered to find cedar branches, and urged the girls yet again to buy the other piñata which, as we already mentioned, looked like a general.

This peddler, an old man dressed in rags, was well known at police headquarters, Belén Prison, and the Hospital de San Pablo. The doctors there were familiar with his innards and his brains, and looked upon Anselmo (as he was called) with scientific interest, for on two occasions this drunkard miraculously recovered from grave injuries, the first time to his stomach and the second time to his head.

Lupe and Otilia were kind to Anselmo, and for a good reason: these girls were quite happy and contented . . . and the curious reader will eventually understand why they felt so good and were so full of generosity and other virtues.

The house had a spacious kitchen. A clever and well-educated young engineer had designed it so that it would have a brick oven. It's true that as far as its hearth was concerned, this kitchen, like all Mexican kitchens, dated back over three hundred years. The bellows still triumphed over scientific truths concerning the weight of air and the production of calories; and that was because the engineer, following the instructions of his aunt, had the oven built in the traditional style.

There were four servants, two of whom revealed, by their wretched appearance, that they had been hired off the street for this occasion.

Abstinence, penance, and mortification of the flesh were taken in jest in that kitchen. Virtue was in costume and arm-in-arm with Gluttony, as during Carnival; both had come to celebrate this prodigious event in Christendom. Lucullus* and Heliogabalus,† eager to attend the party, entered through the kitchen. After many months, the codfish and sea bass were given a cold bath; and the servants cleaned rosemary leaves, condemning millions of generations of insects to oblivion by piling the eggs to one side. Little figures were carved into white slices of jícama, which would be stained red by the beets in the Christmas Eve salad. This classic and traditional salad, which mixes together an assortment of fruits and vegetables, has lent its name to literary sketches and fraternal orders. It brings good cheer to the guests; and as the prosody of this family supper, it is keenly missed by the dead.

Lupe and Otilia opened the door for two delivery men who carried crates filled with wines and canned food from Quintín

---

* Lucullus (c. 110 B.C. – 56 B.C.), Roman general famous for his sumptuous lifestyle.

† Heliogabalus (c. 205 A.D.– 222 A.D.), Roman emperor notorious for his gluttony.

Gutiérrez. After these tins of fish and wine bottles had been un-
packed, they found a slip of paper which said: "Compliments of
General N—— for No. 2, ——Street. Gutiérrez."

There were now two people who had hitched their fortunes to
the General: the piñata peddler and Quintín Gutiérrez.

III

We entered that house through the kitchen; and we are fond of giving all things their due.

Not all houses are entered through the salon, nor is the salon the principal room in every house. In the house that concerns us, the salon was ordinarily of little importance. But on Christmas Eve, it would become the principal room because there was going to be a ball. Its moment had arrived, and it was to be made anew.

With the liberties granted to authors, we shall continue to give all things their due, and will now proceed from the kitchen to the dining room.

Anselmo the peddler and an army sergeant were arranging cypress boughs on the walls and placing straw all around. The room now had the solemnity of a dark forest, and was well suited for this night of chills and mists, of memories and hopes, and, above all, illusions. The moist air was steeped in the resinous fragrance of evergreens, and it smelled and tasted of Christmas Eve.

There was a room between the dining room and the bedroom that had assumed a variety of uses and services. Here visitors were received, clothes were made, food was stored, and secrets were whispered. The room was open, like a vestibule, in contrast to the adjoining bedroom, which neither the sergeant nor anyone else could enter.

The servants, who use a peculiar nomenclature, didn't simply call it "the bedroom," even though it was the only one in the house. Instead, it was known as "the lady's room."

Once again asserting our privileges as writers, we shall tiptoe inside this room, which for many people had a certain mysterious air, for no apparent reason (at least on the surface).

First of all, beneath a muslin canopy there was the traditional brass bed, which flaunted a thick, fluffy mattress and blue satin sheets concealed by a filigree curtain. The satin and the filigree together had something of the comic nature of bashfulness, which covers its eyes with its hands while keeping its fingers spread.

The celestial blue of the bedroom didn't detract, however, from the earthly scent of magnolia blossoms.

Silence reigned. One walked quietly, because the rug was so soft; and one spoke quietly . . . without knowing why. The French doors opened quietly; they didn't squeak as the front door did. One sat quietly on bedsprings and goose down.

In front of a wide armoire with three mirrors stood "the lady of the house" (as she was called by the sergeant on down).

She was examining her waist in that eloquent monologue of the dressing room, where secrets are kept much better by women than men.

Judging from her back and arms, this woman was young, delicate, and quite pale. With her fingertips, she pinched the sides of her waist to see if its contours could be reduced by another quarter inch.

It is not important to determine whether a woman has learned to draw at a school, because an unsalaried teacher takes every opportunity to correct her lines. She may not know how to draw on paper, but she knows how to make adjustments in front of a mirror.

These corrections took a long time, and absorbed her to such a degree that not even the noise from the rest of the house distracted her, from which we can gather that her first concern was to correct her waistline.

We grow tired of waiting, however, and shall withdraw from this room, hoping for a more opportune moment to introduce our readers to the lady of the house.

IV

W hile the Christmas Eve salad was being prepared in the kitchen, outside the General's "hoose" a veritable salad of guests was being assembled. In certain homes, the guests do not come from that intimate circle of family relations who so grace the domestic hearth, but instead are composed of a hodgepodge of individuals who install themselves for an entire day, quite content because they have some place to go.

From the moment we began to suspect that the General wasn't a real general, and the house was not "his" house, these guests were thrown into a questionable light that makes it difficult for us to introduce them to our readers. We hardly know Lupe and Otilia, but our ignorance is quite understandable since no one in that house could give us any details about their parentage. We must go elsewhere in search of information.

Lupe was the daughter of a government paymaster, of the sort who pays others for six months of the year and then, when least expected, pays the rest to himself. He had made this kind of formal payment twice, and as a result, had become so servile and obliging in the General's house that he let Lupe do whatever she pleased there, especially when it meant being of service to the young lady who was correcting her waist at the end of the last chapter.

Lupe was eighteen years old, petite, and, of course, anemic. Her complexion had that shade of blotting paper retained by the mixed race when its Aztec copper is rinsed away. Lupe battled constantly with her color, which explains why she wore a hat with a very large white plume. Her hair was black and cut in a straight line over her eyebrows to form what she called her "fringe."

No one knew who her mother was; it was only known that her father was the paymaster. But that didn't matter; Lupe was able to change circles thanks to some friends she met while attending the Conservatory of Music for six months.

Otilia was one of the friends Lupe made at that school, and in much the same way, Otilia made friends with a student at the Preparatory School—the young man with the dark moustache who had nowhere to celebrate the posadas.

Lupe, who had already acquired certain rights in the General's house, arranged it so that this boyfriend could spend Christmas Eve there.

That's why Otilia was jumping for joy.

Otilia's complexion wasn't as dark as Lupe's, and she was taller, but they were about the same age. She knew how to dress fashionably, and also had a hat with a white plume. That hat and the student from the Preparatory School were the two things that made her happy.

"Tell me," she said to Lupe, full of gratitude, "what more could I want? I have my white hat and my boyfriend. Is there anything else?"

"Does he love you?"

"Love me! You should see the poems he's written. He says they're positivist poems. Mama won't look at them because she says he's a heretic."

"All mothers say the same thing. If a boyfriend doesn't go to confession, forget about it! They think he's already condemned."

"Tell me, does the General go to confession?"

"Not the General again! You bad girl!"

"And you're so secretive. But I already know about—"

"About what?"

"About the white shoes you're going to wear tonight—he bought them for you."

"Well, what's wrong with that? White shoes must be worn, and you know my poor father can't afford them. But the General is so kind that, to my surprise, a servant came in with a basket, saying, 'See if these fit,' and . . . what else could I do? The only thing bothering me was not having proper shoes for tonight."

"Well, I've got a pair, too."

"From the student?"

"Heaven forbid!"

"From your mama?"

"Not from her, either. To tell you the truth, I'm paying Don Mateo by installments."

"We'll look like princesses tonight in our shoes!"

At that moment the paymaster entered.

"My papa," Lupe said.

He had been making arrangements for the musicians. He pushed his hat back and sat down in an armchair.

"I told the General that the musicians would cost him plenty if we didn't hire them early enough. Now they want forty pesos."

"Come closer!" a silvery voice shouted out from the bedroom.

Well before the paymaster made any payments to himself, ugliness had paid a larger tribute to him. His coppery skin, his bristly black moustache, and his crewcut preserved his military style despite his black suit and tie. The African race could still be detected in the angles of his face, which explained why he kept his hair so short, because when he was an army private and assistant to the General, the troops gave him the nickname "Curly." Ever since then, the General hasn't called him anything else.

Once again, the silvery voice of the "lady" reverberated from behind the French doors.

"What is Curly saying?"

"The musicians want forty pesos," he answered.

"So?"

"That's very expensive."

"But you're only making the arrangements."

"Yes, I know it's the General who's paying, but I think it's too much."

"Too much? Why? Those poor musicians! It's only fair they should earn something on Christmas Eve. It only comes once a year."

The paymaster shrugged his shoulders. After a little while, he stood up and asked:

"So I'll hire them?"

"Yes," the voice answered.

"Those are your orders?"

"Yes, my orders."

And he left without saying another word.

V

A s we have not yet had a chance to take a good look at the lady of the house, we shall provide some details about her person. Some years ago, there was a very well-known figure in Mexico, the mere mention of whose name would save us from providing his biography. We shall, however, discreetly conceal his identity and give him the common name of Pancho, which was what his friends called him. Pancho was in the military, and the life he led there was a tapestry of sudden reversals, travels, transformations, and adventures, a fate shared by an incredible number of individuals whose way of life is tied to the agitation and public tumult our country has experienced for so many years.

Not surprisingly, he was ruined by the first interregnum of peace; he had the sort of personality that only thrives during revolutions. He couldn't serve in the permanent army for a few very compelling reasons: he was lazy, full of vices, and had been court-martialed, although he made it seem as though the latter was due to the implacable hatred of the Ministry of War.

"Look at what the Ministry has done to me," Pancho said to

begin with; and then after showing many documents that no one read, ended by asking for a peso.

He eventually died in abject poverty, leaving several children behind. These did not form a single family, but, rather, were scattered and far-flung. One daughter of Pancho's was taken in by some distant aunts, and by age fifteen she had already tasted of life's bitterness, from abandonment to hunger and even dishonor.

Never has the importance of maternal warmth in shaping the hearts of children been more evident than in this present case. A mother puts countless drops of sweetness into our souls and plants God knows how many seeds of purity, which unite us with goodness for the rest of our lives. Pancho's daughter was virtuous because of circumstances, not principles, and as soon as she could lift a corner of the veil that conceals life's pleasures, she escaped like a captive animal through the first crack of light.

Ever since then, this girl has been one of those parasites whose numbers are increasing at an alarming rate in modern society, presenting the sociological sciences with difficult, insoluble problems respecting the welfare of the people.

Once outside the warp woven by morality, by maternal love, by an education based on observation and experience, and by a social contract anchored in philosophical ideas, a woman goes forth in the world as part of an immense guild whose members live by their own devices, having broken with the principles of morality, the institution of the family, and the destiny of women.

A terrible philosophy has flooded our present society through the dikes of science and morality. Its disciples populate the big cities around the world and, with their red fingernails, open a deep abyss into which the public wealth disappears.

What we now call "these ladies" were once referred to as "those women." Let us agree, then, that modern society, which is less demanding and meticulous, if you will, has quite willingly cleared a wide path for this invading brigade.

These brief notes allow us to better understand the physiognomy of "the lady of the house." If the reader meditates on the lines we have traced, he will discover the sort of character upon which the picture of beauty may be printed, and will realize that in our day photography has made such progress that a negative can be printed on stone as well as steel.

The moment has arrived to reveal that the lady of the house is none other than the daughter of that panhandling soldier, Pancho. Her name is Julia, although we aren't sure if that is her real name. Carried along by the terrible flood we just mentioned, she landed in the General's arms amidst the cool shade of peacetime and the heat of the National Treasury.

VI

J ulia was what is called a fashionable beauty. She had the
medium height of the meridional race, and her movements
were suffused by that voluptuous languor belonging to the
woman who lives only to please others. Ever since she broke with
social conventions, she became completely devoted to her own
self-worship. It is not necessary to name the dramas in which she
had played the leading role; but these dramas left behind, much
against her will, traces of a profound, concentrated sadness, above
which her sparkling laughter flashed like lightning over a putrid
swamp.

Her most extravagant flights of fancy arose from the depths of
this sadness. One evening, on December fifteenth to be exact, she
waited for the General to arrive at his habitual time.

"What do you want?" the General asked, before Julia even had
a chance to pronounce her wish.

"Posadas," she answered dryly.

"Posadas. And we're going to pray to the Holy Pilgrims?"

"Why not? And sing the litany. I'm longing to hear your
voice."

"Have you given this any thought?"

"Of course!"

"Posadas for the two of us?"

"Don't play dumb. Do you think I'd be satisfied with only you?"

"What do you mean!"

"We'll have, of course, the traditional gathering."

The General couldn't hide his dismay.

"I understand, General. You're not amused by the idea of having guests. Well, don't worry: I'm not inviting your wife or your daughters; they're so dreary. I don't like those kind of people."

"Then who do you want to invite?" the General asked, biting his lips.

"You'll see. First of all, Lupe and Otilia, those poor girls! They're so excited!"

"Good."

"Good, eh? I see. You'll agree I haven't made a bad choice, especially Lupe."

She accompanied this remark with a hateful look that was immediately followed by a beautiful smile.

The General, anticipating her hostility, lowered his eyes, then raised them to capture her smile. He was an artful strategist and knew the circumstances under which she deployed her sublime tactics.

"And then—" Julia faltered, "and then . . . the two girls across the hall."

"Do you think they'll come?"

"To the posadas? Why wouldn't they?"

"And what about men?"

"Don't you think there are any to invite?"

"Yes, but . . ."

"Yes, but . . ." Julia repeated, mocking him. "You know, you're being very tiresome tonight. Look, to make it short, we're celebrating the posadas, you'll sing the litany with me, I'll give you a candle, we'll break open a piñata, and we'll do whatever else I want, is that clear?"

"All right, Julia, whatever you wish. But as far as I'm concerned, I'd rather be alone with you."

"You're so selfish! Our privacy! I'm bored of it. Your visits are becoming tedious. We need to vary our tactics, General."

Julia got up to check her hair in a mirror. She knew when it was to her advantage to let the General see her in full. As she stood up, she was like a flower suddenly moved by a gust of wind after a long rest: the air was permeated by her perfume, which entered the General's nostrils and initialed an approval to the posadas on his brain.

It is not within our plan to describe the entire posadas, but only the party held on Christmas Eve, the subject of this chronicle.

Julia mentioned "the girls across the hall," and since they will be part of the festivities, we shall introduce them to our readers.

There were four apartments in Julia's building. Opposite her apartment lived the mother of two young ladies and five boys, the seven offspring of a clerk in the Ministry of Finance who, like many trees, had aged prematurely as a result of being pruned too little and bearing too much fruit. For fifteen years, this family had overcome the most intractable of social problems, pauperism, for it grew and multiplied without a corresponding growth and multiplication of income. The portions into which a piece of bread was divided on this couple's honeymoon increased every three hundred and sixty days, with a progressive decrease in the nutrition, warmth, and vitality of the family. The sap ran thinner the further the fruit was from the trunk of the tree, so that Juvencia, the oldest, was the most robust and intelligent; after her came Lola, who was anemic, followed by Pedrito on crutches, then scrawny Juan, Enriqueta who was deaf from typhus, and three sickly boys, the last of whom was consumptive.

Despite the poverty of their household, Juvencia and Lola were presentable on formal occasions such as the posadas at the General's house. Their mother, however, hadn't had much good fortune since the day she was married. A model of self-abnegation and suffering, she had renounced the world without effort and without protest. She was one of those saintly wives who are so plentiful in Mexico, and only in Mexico, for whom marriage is an open coffin from which only the soul escapes on the last day.

She was strongly opposed to her daughters' attending the posadas, but her husband wasn't as scrupulous about these matters because, as he said, he had seen plenty.

"We are not obliged," he said to his wife, "to ask people for their marriage license. In this building, Julia is regarded as the General's wife, and that's how we should treat her."

"Excuse me," answered his wife, who was wrapped in a black shawl. "Let me tell you, there's no one in this building who doesn't know what's going on. Don't you think the neighbors pay close attention to these things?"

"All right, let's say it's true. But the General has invited me personally, and, as you know, I have to stay on good terms with him. He's good friends with Fuentes Muñiz, and I'm not going to risk my job for any twinge of conscience, understand? Also, a very select group has attended these past few nights—two congressmen were there with their wives."

"Who did you say they were with?"

"With their wives."

"Oh, really? As you say, we shouldn't ask people for their marriage license."

"Of course not. In any case, there hasn't been any rowdiness, and all the guests behaved properly. Julia, if you had only seen her, did the honors like a marquise."

"I'm so pleased I won't see her!"

"Yes, I know you have a strong aversion toward her."

"No, what I have is anger toward a society that treats the rules of decorum so lightly."

"My word! Aren't you eloquent tonight! Look, let's stop talking about this and attend the party in peace. What could possibly happen to my daughters if they're with me? Young girls are always safe by their father's side wherever they go."

VII

Julia got just what she wanted. Invitations went out for the Christmas Eve ball, and the General's friends and others would be coming to pay her homage. With that, Julia felt a deep satisfaction that made up for the countless humiliations she had suffered in her life.

One of the best dressmakers in Mexico City delivered her ballgown. It was pale pink with lace and flowers and, without a doubt, would make a perfect contrast to the dresses worn by Lupe and Otilia, and even more so to those worn by the girls across the hall.

The two congressmen who came along with "their wives" didn't attend the posadas for each of the nine evenings, because Julia seemed much too proud to them. But two days before the ball, one of the congressmen discovered that Julia was not as proud as she seemed.

The type of discovery made by the congressmen tends to be more or less transcendental; indeed, the good fortune of the General began to inspire envy.

Something had happened to the General that only he could understand. After meeting Julia, he dusted off among his many trophies the bloom of his youth; he was reinvigorated, and believed he had the perfect right to round out his life with an episode of love. He fully surrendered to this gallant adventure; it seemed the most natural thing in the world to indulge in this whim. But nearly a year had gone by, and he had sampled her bad behavior over a thousand times. His wife and children had become a harsh and continual reproach, and he couldn't put them out of his mind. He tried to exaggerate his wife's faults in order to justify his own actions and, using his business as an excuse, spent as little time at home as possible. As far as his wife and children knew, he had made three trips to León on the new railroad and two trips to Cuautla; and there were more imaginary trips planned to other destinations.

When he was a faithful husband, he was never jealous and lived in peace; but now he had turned into an Othello. The congressmen and the other friends he allowed into Julia's home treated her with a certain *sans façon* that made his blood boil. They spoke too freely in her company and looked at her in an unseemly way.

Faced with such improprieties, the General considered how much this whimsy had cost him, yet he stopped short of confessing he wasn't happy. He missed the peace and quiet that had once seemed so boring. Now it had reached the point where he visited Julia more to guard her than see her. The General, in brief, had embarked on one of those escapades requiring a youthful recklessness that, much to his dismay, he could no longer summon. The naked truth had revealed itself, but, nevertheless, he put up with the situation out of self-respect.

As for Julia, she had never declared her affections; he had rescued her from a delicate, near-terrible predicament, and she took refuge with this interim savior who paid the rent and the dressmaker. But the General was ugly and jealous, and Julia thought of little else besides finding a way to escape from this obligation.

The ideas of the congressman and Julia were about to coincide in this respect, but such matters are best discussed over champagne. Fortunately, Don Quintín Gutiérrez had sent over two crates for Christmas Eve.

VIII

I t is of utmost importance on Christmas Eve to visit the house by way of the kitchen, because there one finds the main attractions of the party, which (like any in Christendom) begins with a hearty appetite.

Expert hands were carrying out all the preliminary operations. A gossipy servant and Anselmo, the peddler, sat beside each other on the same wooden crate. This drudge was cleaning rosemary leaves, and Anselmo was helping her. Their monotonous job allowed them to talk, and us to listen.

"You don't know what's goin' on," Anselmo said sarcastically.

"No? That's what you think."

"Well, I know his other lady. I sweep over there when they need me. Doña Petra, the cook, she's my source."

"So she told you—"

"Well, Doña Petra told me the General was going to León."

"Go on! Is that so, Don Anselmo?"

"I swear it."

"That means the General spends all his time traveling." She began to sing, *"Tonight is Christmas Eve—"*

"—*the night to make buñuelos**—*" another servant croaked.

"—*but in my 'hoose' we can't make 'em,*" Anselmo added, " *'cause we're out of flour and eggs.*"

Everyone laughed at this traditional song, as it well described the present circumstances in the General's house.

"So you're going to tell the cook—" murmured the servant who sang along with Anselmo.

"It's my right, ma'am. We all need t' get by and we each have our way. The poor live off the rich, an' they appreciate me, they know who Anselmo is, an' forgive me for sayin' it, Doña Trinita, but I don't care if I do—"

"So everybody—"

"Now you see."

"Everybody's got to—"

"Like the priest told me, ever'body's got his own consciensh."

"What priest?"

"The one that heard me confess at San Pablo."

"You mean you go to confession!"

"Well no . . . but with my guts spillin' out, Doña Trinita, why not."

"When was that?"

"When I was beat to a pulp."

"Where?"

"In Don Adalid's bar. I almost got killed."

"And you recovered?"

" 'Course I did! The surgeons put me back together—thanks to a needle, Doña Trini, they stitch'd me up like the cover on a ball."

"Heavens, Don Anselmo!"

"We men are tough, my darlin'."

"My *what?* God help me!"

Even though they were cleaning rosemary leaves, their exchange contained all the elements of the drama that inspired the legend of Pyramus and Thisbe.

---

*   A crispy, round wafer made from flour, eggs, and water; the dough is fried in oil and sweetened with honey or sugar. Traditionally prepared during the Christmas season.

Doña Trini (as Anselmo respectfully called her) remained pensive. At that moment, Lupe's father, otherwise known as Curly, stuck his head into the kitchen and asked in a loud voice:

"Where's the General?"

"He's not here," several voices answered.

After he left the kitchen Anselmo said, "A general in a kitchen? What was Curly thinkin' of?"

"How'd you know his name's Curly?" Trini asked.

"I didn't say that's his name — that's what he's called."

"You know everybody, Don Anselmo."

"That's my specialty. If you get around like me. . . . Now take Curly. I know where's he's been. We were in jail together, but when the bosses get out of Belén, they don't want to know your name."

"Isn't Don Anselmo bad!" Trini said to her neighbor. "He says he knew Curly in Tlalpiloya!*"

"No!"

"Believe me, it's true. But don't let Curly hear it, 'cause now he's good friends with the police, and they can make trouble for you."

"I saw him with Don Narciso, the gendarme," a servant said.

"Drinking tequila, of course."

"I didn't see that."

"Don Narciso is always drunk," Trini said, "the other night he yanked me so hard my rebozo would've ripped, except I was wearing this heavy one."

"When was that?"

"When I went to get some bread for the missus."

"Everybody was drunk that night."

"Even the General," the cook whispered, cupping her mouth with her hands.

"Be quiet, Doña Lola, the missus might hear you . . ."

"What then?"

"She'll get even."

"So what? The girls who work on Calle de Arco are dying for me to cook for them. Over there they give you enough to go to the puppet show, and they go to sleep early, not like here — here

* Popular name for Belén Prison.

144

all you get is some champagne and then . . . forget about it! It's three or four in the morning, and you're still on your feet!"

"Don't even mention champagne, Doña Lola. I swear, when I hear corks pop, I get gas pains."

Curly looked in the salon for the General to report on one of the hundred tasks he had performed.

"Is the General here?" he shouted.

"He's not here," Julia answered loudly. "What do you want?"

"I want to tell him Señor Pinechet wasn't at home, and Don Antonio can't make it because he has a cold, but the girls will do their best to come for a little while."

"So who's coming, in the end?" Julia said impatiently.

"The two congressmen and the ladies, and Rosalitos."

"Ah yes, I knew Rosalitos was coming, he's a close friend of the General's and he's . . . a fine man. I'm so glad he's coming."

Now there were two people Julia would be pleased to see that night: first, one of the congressmen, and second, Rosalitos.

IX

The early hours of the evening slowly passed by while countless preparations were made.

Curly and Otilia placed stearine candles in the candalabras.

Lupe was busy at her dressing table and, at the same time, in the dining room. The ranks of the kitchen staff were increased by two or three boys from the neighborhood who had asked the cook if there were any odd jobs. They were immediately put to work shelling peanuts and chopping fruit for the Christmas Eve salad. Julia was making grand preparations in front of her mirror. Using both hands, she rubbed cream onto her face for over an hour. She also perfected what a friend called "finishing touches" for this special night, which meant drawing a very thin black line under her lower eyelid, and painting her lips with a red lipstick she had received as a gift.

The first guest arrived at nine o'clock: it was Otilia's boyfriend. Otilia greeted him in the vestibule because the rest of the house was still dark and in disarray.

To her boyfriend, the darkness seemed like a luminous idea.

Otilia thought the darkness suited her, since she hadn't dressed for the ball yet, and this way she would make a greater impression on her boyfriend when he saw her in full light. Their conversation was interrupted by two servants from Fulcheri's Restaurant who came laden with pastries for the table.

Around ten o'clock, while an army sergeant was lighting the lamps and candles, the musicians arrived. It took two of them to carry the double bass indoors.

A double bass and a pretty woman are always greeted with a smile. I've yet to meet a person who is so serious that he can keep a straight face when a double bass goes by; not because this instrument is funny in itself, but because it always appears on formal occasions, and announces a merry program.

"Here comes the bull fiddle!" some of the girls in the kitchen shouted. Lupe and Otilia gazed at it while smacking their lips at the thought of dancing. The dandy from the Preparatory School couldn't stop thinking of Otilia's waist, and even Curly felt his feet grow lighter despite all the walking the General had made him do that day.

By this time, Julia was finished with her toilette. She couldn't resist looking at the double bass, which the musicians, afraid of damaging the wall hangings, had rested on its side in the salon.

The salon was all lit up and empty. Otilia's boyfriend stayed in the vestibule.

Julia, with the long train of her pale pink dress trailing behind her, entered the salon to contemplate this stringed instrument. She had never had a double bass at her feet before, nor seen one close up, and she interrogated it as if waiting for its three greased strings to respond. To her it seemed that this cetacea of the musical world had deliberately prostrated itself to pay her homage. There it lay humiliated, just like the General. Everything that evening was a result of her work, her determination, her caprice; she had tangible proof of her dominion. The double bass spoke silently to her pride before speaking melodiously of love to the guests.

Julia couldn't help but have tender feelings toward this instrument. She raised the skirt of her dress and plucked one of its strings with the toe of her dazzlingly white satin shoe.

The double bass let out a kind of muted roar that made her shudder. She dropped the hem of her skirt and turned around to see if anyone had been watching.

Otilia's boyfriend, who observed this scene through the glass panes of the French doors, stepped back so that she wouldn't see him. He didn't think it was the best moment to be introduced.

Julia left the double bass and went over to the mirror for a final inspection.

A moment later, the visitors entered and made their own introductions. The ladies accompanied their greeting with a peculiar notion of an embrace, which consisted of placing their fingertips on each other's shoulders.

Julia knew hardly any of these people. As predicted, the gathering was turning into another kind of Christmas Eve salad. How could it have been otherwise?

Two young men came into the room and approached Julia with a determined air. One of them extended his arm and squeezed her hand familiarly, saying:

"Let me introduce—"

There was a burst of laughter. Julia and the man being introduced already knew each other.

"Oh! So you two—"

"Well, well!" her old acquaintance said.

He sat down beside her while his friend went off with their coats.

"Don't start with one of your—" Julia said.

"You look so beautiful tonight! You wear the General's sash so well!"

"How dare you!"

"Now it's you who's starting with me."

"Who told you I was having a ball?"

"Perico."

"Listen to me—do you know what the General's like?"

"On the battlefield, but not in the barracks. Does he get jealous?"

"You devil!"

"Does he?"

"Yes, for God's sake."

"Then let's dance tonight, you and I! Just like in Guadalajara."

"You're crazy."

"I'm crazy about how that sash fits you."

The musicians came in, stood the double bass upright, and brandished a trombone, a violin, a cornet, and a flute.

The double bass let out the same dull roar that Julia had produced with her foot, and she was reminded of what had taken place shortly before.

After tuning their instruments, the musicians realized that the guests were not yet ready to dance, so they began playing the overture to *William Tell.*

Neither the congressmen, the General, nor Rosalitos had made their appearance yet.

X

The salon was aglow. A pair of candalabras with twenty-four candles (bought at an auction by the General) radiated shafts of light that picked up the metallic glint of the gold and white wallpaper, and threw a cascade of silver threads onto Julia's pale pink dress. The stearine candles seemed to aim their rays deliberately at the eyelids of the queen of the ball, and those rays, like doves perched on a marble cornice, cast a shadow onto her eyes that complemented the black line that she had drawn under her lower lid for the first time.

Unbeknownst to Julia, this fortuitous light gave her eyes a value beyond price. The depths of their passion and fire were such that her gaze, which was normally intense and calculating, now had a mysterious, irresistible power. Such is the influence of the lightest touch of the master hand on a line drawn under an eye; such is the effect of a charcoal line and a hint of candlelight on the poor sons of Adam. We openly confess: that night, due to a combination of small details that would otherwise have gone unnoticed, Julia's eyes were capable, like an evil genie, of leading souls down the road to sin. Which is to say that Curly, that servile, inoffensive factotum of the house, was struck dumb as he looked at Julia; he contemplated her for such a long time that she couldn't help but ask:

"Why are you looking at me?"

"Who, me?"

"Yes."

"Well, you see, the truth is—" he said, running the fingers of his right hand through his hair, "the truth is . . . you'll be angry with me, but—"

"Come on, what is it? For God's sake, say what's on your mind."

"Just say it?"

"Yes, yes, yes!"

"Well, the truth, the truth is, you're very beautiful tonight."

"Really?"

"I swear it."

"Hmm, and what's so beautiful about me?" Julia asked while using both hands to open a fan made of marabou feathers.

"What can I say that won't make you laugh at me? And I . . . I . . ."

The paymaster seemed overwhelmed.

"And it's—" he continued, "it's such a pleasure to look at you."

"I can tell. And what do you think of my dress?" Julia asked, prompting him.

"That's not the only thing—that dress makes you look like a queen, but the truth is, there's something else . . ."

"Something else? What, then?"

"Something else that is making me . . . very sad."

"Sad! What do you mean?"

"Yes, the truth is, I'm sad."

"But what's making you sad, my dear Curly?"

Her "my dear Curly" sent shivers down his spine: it was uttered by Julia's red lips and passed through the feathers of her fan, which she had drawn close to her mouth. Her perfumed breath, along with a flood of other scents, reached his dark nostrils, making that poor devil's nervous system vibrate like an electrical current. He grew pale and swallowed the sentence that was in his throat.

Julia, who had stepped closer to him to say "my dear Curly," observed his reactions, and with the quick insight that only women possess on such occasions, understood him, and pretended at the same time not to have noticed a thing. But she was surprised to learn that "my dear Curly" was the key to some unexpected feelings of her own.

"I always treat this poor fellow badly," Julia thought "and now that I've called him 'my dear Curly' he's quite moved. He thinks he's far beneath me . . . I'm fine, thank you." Her thoughts were interrupted by the entrance of the congressmen and Rosalitos, who greeted her.

"You're dazzling," one of the congressmen said.

"Be dazzled, then," Julia answered with a wink.

"You're so elegant tonight," the other one added.

"That's what someone just told me, but I don't want to believe it."

"You know, the lady General looks scrumptious tonight!" one of the dandies said to another, confident that his description had hit the mark.

"You think so?"

"Yes, I do! And I'm going to ask her for a dance."

"I bet you won't."

"You'll see." He approached Julia. "Will I be so lucky as to have the next dance with you, miss?"

"Which one?"

"The one after this."

Julia looked at him for a few moments. The dandy trembled until she nodded her assent.

"Thank you," he said, as if he had been awarded first prize in mathematics.

"And which dance is mine?" asked the favored congressman, that is, the one we said had discovered that Julia was not as proud as she seemed.

At that moment, the music began.

Julia took the congressman's arm . . . and the General entered the salon. Curly, after a long soliloquy that concluded on a gloomy note, went into the dining room to uncork the first bottle of cognac. Poor Curly! He found refuge in the cognac like a dog in garbage.

As to the congressman, he was holding a secret legislative session with Julia as they danced check-to-cheek. She approved the first measure on his agenda and dispensed with the necessary formalities. When she passed close to the General, who couldn't hide his displeasure, she said:

"What a surprise! I thought you weren't coming." And without waiting for an answer, she made a half-turn away from him.

The congressman cast his vote with a tiny squeeze of her hand, and Julia seconded the motion.

He was slightly taller than Julia and had a goatee. Before the ball, he went to have his hair combed, and that rascal of a barber used a handful of Hungarian pomade to make his beard come to a point; and this point was so firm and silky that it tickled the epidermis of Julia's left shoulder, such that she had twice felt, as she put it, "the little death."

Like a diver for pearls, Julia had gathered two notable impressions on her first dive: Curly's paleness, and the tip of the congressman's beard.

The room had somehow filled with people. Guests came in and, without ceremony, blended into the crowd. There were people in the vestibule, in the hallway, in Julia's bedroom, all over the house. At first, the General was surprised to be so honored, but then he suddenly realized that his was a secondary role; he knew hardly anyone there. He regretted having yielded to Julia's wishes. With great difficulty, he walked through the crowd into the dining room, guided by the same idea that had brought Curly there. The General found Curly standing in front of a bottle of cognac and a glass.

"Have a little cognac, General."

The General stretched out his arm. Curly filled the glass halfway and handed it to him. Without a word, the General took a few gulps and turned to look around him. He contemplated the whole spectacle: the servants from Fulcheri's, the crates with abundant wine, plates, and glasses, and the multitudes of people who were either giving orders or carrying them out. Before thinking about Julia and her fantasy, he remembered the moneylender to whom he had signed over his next paycheck, and the two overdrafts he had made. These last, somewhat bitter ingredients had not been considered in the Christmas Eve salad.

Meanwhile, Lupe and Otilia had the chance to enjoy themselves. Neither Otilia's mother nor anyone else in her family was at the party; only the student from the Preparatory School was there, and he and Otilia had already danced twice.

After she finished her dance, Julia neither waited on the General nor carried out any of the domestic duties that corresponded to the "lady of the house." The ball was for her, and she made the most of whatever gave her pleasure. The congressman, who made sure to sit beside Julia, issued his expert opinion on a pair of eyes that a charcoal line and the lights from the candelabra had made so interesting.

The candelabra continued to send a shower of gold over Julia. Her satin dress shot off bolts of lightning that illuminated the congressman's face and doubled the eloquence of his words. Yet Julia, lacking as she was in real feelings (which had been squandered through use), showed the childlike interest a woman of the world has in the smallest details. She trained her eyes on the shadow that the point of the congressman's beard cast onto the wide expanse of his shirtfront.

The General returned from the dining room and stopped in front of Julia. She regarded him for a few moments, then finally broke the silence that was becoming awkward.

"I see you're in a bad mood."

"No, I'm not," said the General, with a tone and posture that corroborated Julia's remark.

The congressman, with utmost diplomacy, offered his seat to the General, who accepted it without a word of thanks.

"All right, then," Julia said. "So this is your idea of pleasing me. Have you been fighting with your wife? Well, if she put you in a bad mood, it's not fair to take it out on me. Understand?"

"It's because—"

"It's because—you're so tiresome."

"That's become your favorite word."

"I'm not to blame."

"Well, who's to blame, then?"

"You. You feel guilty whenever you do something for me. It's very simple . . . Look at how pretty I am tonight, dummy."

Someone approached Julia at this inopportune moment to ask her for a waltz.

The General was stung by Julia's words, and was plunged into a sea of misgivings that darkened his spirits even further. He was beginning to understand the full magnitude of this adventure which, as we have already said, required a youthful recklessness that the General could no longer muster, not even after drinking the finest cognac.

XI

In that salon, more than in any other, the social graces and cultivation of the guests could be judged by their behavior. When the
music stopped playing, the room began to clear; all the men moved
away from the center of the party to station themselves in the adjoining rooms or in the hallway, avoiding any contact or conversation
with the older ladies. These, in turn, occupied all the chairs and
stayed quietly in their seats during the breaks, turning to each other
only to criticize and whisper in gossipy tones about the other women.

The object of any gathering in respectable society is to make
conversation, to interact with others, to strengthen superficial
bonds, and to develop existing friendships and form new ones.
Balls, concerts, and dinners are simply a means, not an end in
themselves. A person whose culture is far from refined attends a
ball only to dance, and a dinner only to eat. The reason the room
cleared whenever a dance ended was because the two sexes are
like oil and water: shaken together by the rhythm of the music,
they separate as soon as the music stops.

There was not a single young man, no matter how brazen he
was on the street, who would dare to cross the dance floor

by himself. To do so would have entailed an almost painful sacrifice.

After one long interlude, the boldest young men, spurred on by the degree of enthusiasm inspired by a certain young lady, encouraged one another to cross to the other side of the room, which was festooned with ladies.

"Suárez, come with me."

"Why?"

"To walk across the room to ask Chole for the next dance."

"No, my friend, I wouldn't dare. Wait until the music starts."

"Let's go right now."

"No."

"Why not?"

"If you only knew how mortified I am to cross the floor."

"It's the same for me, too."

"It always feels like a mile."

"My legs tremble."

"Mine don't, but I feel like I'm walking on eggshells."

"What happens to me is that I ask for the next dance, they say yes, and then I can't think of anything else to say. I'm struck dumb after I say thank you, and I have to cross the floor again. Then I imagine all the women are criticizing the way I walk, my tie, my boots, or something."

"Or your sideburns."

"There you go again about my sideburns! You'll see, just wait until next year."

While the young men herded together in the vestibule and around the doorways, the older women began finding fault.

"Who is she?" a fat lady asked her daughter. "That one with the blue bow?"

"She lives in this building. Her name is Juvencia, and she attends the National School."

"Did you know, Juanita," one old lady said to another, "that I don't care much for the lady of the house?"

"Why is that, Doña Gualupita?"

"Because . . . first, she's not as pretty as they say—she's wearing a lot of makeup."

"Well, you already know that they all—"

"Yes, I can see that, and some of them look like rats in a bakery. And second," the old lady continued, "she has a way of sitting down. . . . Look at her now, but don't let her see you. It's true she has lovely feet and beautiful shoes, but she shows them too much. Don't you agree?"

"Yes, I noticed that already. But I know something worse."

"What's that?"

"She's not the General's real wife."

"That can't be true. You know how people gossip. No, as far as that's concerned, I'm convinced she's his real wife. If not, would I have allowed my daughters to come?"

"That's what they say. And there's even more—some know his wife and daughters."

"Well, they're mistaken. The other woman is the one who's not his real wife."

"Be quiet! How strange!"

"Yes, isn't it mysterious."

During this short exchange, four young dandies finally set out on their journey across the dance floor. Following them was the rest of the herd, ready to take their partners when the musicians began to play.

At about half past eleven, Curly began to uncork several bottles and had dozens of glasses sent round as aperitifs. These drinks spread their influence throughout the salon, and the voices grew louder and louder. A few young men even dared to stand in groups in the middle of the floor.

The second time the congressman danced with Julia, their poetry was so eloquent that the General cast his veto with the following two words:

"Sit down."

But Julia, who wouldn't submit, responded at first with a coquettish gesture, and then, after the General's second notice, with a tantrum. The General spoke into the congressman's ear:

"Take her to a seat."

He said this in such a brusque tone that the congressman obeyed, but not without a look of protest.

When Julia realized that the congressman was leading her to a chair, she exclaimed:

"I can't stand cowards!"

She freed herself from the congressman's arm and approached the father of the girls who lived across the way. She said in an unusually pleasant and sweet tone:

"Do you want to have a little dance with me?"

This poor clerk, who couldn't dance and had hardly ever spoken to Julia before, could barely get a word out; but Julia had already taken his hand and pushed aside another couple standing in front of them. He was so spellbound that he didn't know what he was doing: with the palm of his right hand, he felt her satin dress, and with his left, the touch of Julia's hand. An intoxicating torrent of fragrances rose from her breast as from the calyx of a magnolia. He thought he was dreaming and moved almost unconsciously to the rhythm of the music; he felt agile, light-footed, and entirely at home on the dance floor. How strange! The last time he danced with his wife, he ripped her dress and stepped on her twice, but now he felt like a born dancer. He was short, shorter than Julia, and at times the petals of the gardenias she was wearing on her chest brushed against his nose and tickled him. He was attracted as a bee to honey. It was a new and strange sensation for him, one that he had never experienced before. With each turn of the waltz, he felt the gardenia petals tickling him, and was seized by an urge to kiss them. As soon as this temptation entered his head, his lips followed through, and he kissed the flowers without Julia or anyone else noticing.

Suddenly he heard a voice behind him saying:

"Look, look at how excited my papa is!"

"Well done, papa!" another voice added. "What a miracle!"

The clerk was afraid that his daughters had seen his kisses.

When the dance ended, he led Julia to a seat, and thanked her with an expression that rivaled the one she wore when she asked him to dance. He immediately retreated to the dining room to be alone with his feelings and to savor them at his leisure. There he found Curly, the official cupbearer, who offered him a cognac. He was very grateful to Curly, and, as he didn't want to drink alone, they both drank together.

What a coincidence! The General, Curly, the congressman and the clerk were all inspired to drink cognac as a result of the feelings Julia had awaken in each.

While Julia was dancing with the clerk, the General and the congressman spoke with a certain reserve in the adjoining room we mentioned earlier, which was a kind of vestibule destined for many different uses.

After Julia had danced, she went to her bedroom, and from this distance she could see the General and the congressman standing off to the side, engaged in conversation. At that moment, the clock struck twelve. The guests entered the dining room, where supper awaited them.

Neither the congressman nor the General sat next to Julia. Somehow, she suddenly found herself sitting between Curly and the clerk. She realized that something serious was brewing, but, as fickle as she was, she paid more attention to the clerk's gallantries and Curly's flattery than she did to the General. Before long the festive mood spread, and high spirits reigned in the dining room. These high spirits gave way to some confusion as several guests who were half-finished yielded their places to others who hadn't eaten yet.

It was during this moment that the congressman and the General vanished. Their disappearance went unnoticed by Julia.

While the guests were eating, more or less, an interesting scene was taking place in the kitchen.

"Listen, Doña Trinidad," Anselmo said with a mysterious air to the woman who had been cleaning the rosemary leaves, "you said you knew Don Narciso, the gendarme."

"Yes."

"And where is he now?"

"Why?"

"We may need 'im."

"What! You mean—"

"It's serious, Doña Trini. I was in the patio listenin' to the General and th' other gentleman . . . they were havin' a dispute."

"So?"

"Well, they're gonna shoot it out."

"Don't tell me that, Don Anselmo!"

"I swear it."

"When? Here, in this house?"

"No, they left already."

"But they're eating!"

"No, Doña Trini. The General and the other they say's a congressman left along with Rosalitos and another man. It was four that went, and I think it's got somethin' to do with a duel."

"May the Blessed Virgin save us, Don Anselmo!"

"That's why I told you it'd be good to let the gendarme know."

"Don't tell anyone. I'll see if he's downstairs, because he may be off-duty."

Doña Trinidad left the kitchen to look for the gendarme.

Anselmo was right: the General and the congressman were going to fight a duel at sunrise. Their seconds were the other congressman and Rosalitos.

XII

After finishing their meal, some of the guests left the table, and Julia soon discovered that the General and the congressman were absent. Their sudden departure annoyed her deeply. She looked around for a familiar face, and found none other than Curly's.

"What happened to the General?" she asked.

"What! Why are you asking?" Curly said, surprised.

"He left."

"Really! I didn't see . . . I wasn't paying attention . . . "

Indeed, ever since Julia called him "my dear Curly," he had been in a kind of ecstasy. He had eyes only for her, and wasn't aware of what was happening around him.

"Find out what happened—right now," Julia ordered.

Curly searched through the entire house. He looked for the General's coat and hat and finally asked the servants.

He got nowhere at first, and then finally Anselmo told him what they knew in the kitchen.

Julia waited anxiously in her bedroom for Curly's news. When he told her what he had found out, she couldn't contain her fury, and ripped the plumed fan in her hands to shreds. She stared at Curly, and he began to feel the disastrous influence of an electromagnetic surge that caused lustful visions to frolic in his dark, often humiliated soul. His hair, instead of standing on end, became even curlier, as if the sparks thrown off by Julia's eyes were the burning white-hot rays of the Central African sun that had curled the hair of his ancestors some ten generations before. His ignited response was an oasis for Julia in the midst of her tribulations.

"They're having a duel!" she exclaimed when she finished looking at Curly. "A duel! How can that be? How could the congressman fight a duel if he wasn't brave enough to dance with me after the General forbade it? And the General won't fight, either, because he's too old and doesn't love me. Bring me some champagne."

Curly quickly brought back a bottle of champagne and a glass.

"And why did you bring only one glass, stupid! Do you think I'm going to drink all by myself? Are you my servant?"

A servant from Fulcheri's heard Julia and brought another glass.

"Drink, my dear Curly, drink with me and you'll see . . ."

Curly, trembling, gulped down his drink.

Julia laughed when she heard Curly's white teeth chattering against the glass of champagne. The fact that Julia had addressed him familiarly did away with whatever peace of mind he had left. His luck was so great that he was practically speechless. And how strange! For a moment, Julia was awash with a true and profound emotion as well, as if she were in love for the first time. To look upon the brutish Curly, who was trembling and beside himself, was for her a triumph to savor with delight. His ugliness and his coarse, common appearance had a mythological charm for her: she was enveloped by the same atmosphere breathed by satyrs and nymphs in the forest.

Julia grabbed Curly, and they spun onto the dance floor, blending in with the other twirling couples. For twenty minutes she danced with Curly, leading him with her arms, wrapping him in the long train of her pale pink gown, and brushing his face with the petals of her gardenias, which were saturated with an English perfume.

When she sat down, she exclaimed in the most cordial and innocent tone imaginable:

"Hey, girls, let's break the piñatas!"

"Which one?" Lupe asked. "The bride or the general?"

"The bride? Forget about the bride—she's too ugly. Bring out the general!"

"General Boomaboom, General Boomaboom," some of the more outspoken young dandies shouted.

"Bring out the general, my dear Curly, the general," Julia repeated in Curly's ear. "Look, put a blindfold on me but leave one eye uncovered. I want to give the general a good smack on his ribcage. I'm going to challenge him to a duel with sticks—you'll see how I clobber him. All I need is one good swing to knock his stuffing out."

The piñata was brought into the room, and the guests, who had been somewhat reserved while dancing, expressed their utmost joy and excitement. By this time, Otilia and the student from the Preparatory School had disappeared.

Meanwhile, in another house not far from Julia's, a quiet scene of a distinctly different order was taking place. At an unusually early hour, the door leading from the dining room to the kitchen was opened. The lady of the house, a woman in her forties whose face showed all the telltale signs of sleeplessness and distress, was preparing to go outside.

"Good morning, m'lady," the cook said while removing the cover from a burner. "It's early for you to be coming into the kitchen. Do you feel sick?"

"No, Petra, I feel the same as always."

And the lady daubed at her tears with a handkerchief.

"Don't cry, m'lady," Petra said gently. "God willing, it'll turn out for the best."

"Don't believe that, Petra. Did you find something out today?"

"Me?"

"Yes. Since early this morning I've been listening to you talk to the streetsweeper."

"That's true, ma'am, Don Anselmo came very early and we were talking."

"What did Anselmo say?"

"I . . . I don't like to gossip, but you hear certain things . . . and since m'lady asks me every day . . ."

"If I ask you it's because I need to know what's happening. . . . What do you know?"

"Well I . . . I mean, Don Anselmo says that the master . . . I don't know if it's true, because you know how people lie."

"What did he say?"

"He said the master left there around four o'clock with some other gentlemen, well, with three gentlemen to be exact, and that . . ."

"What?"

"Like I told m'lady, it can't be true, because Don Anselmo said he heard something about a duel."

"A duel! Between whom? How? Tell me everything you know."

"Well, not much, just that they left the ball to look for swords and carriages, and that Don Anselmo could hear everything from the kitchen and the patio because it was dark; but I tell you, m'lady, it can't be true."

"Whether it's true or not, I can't stand this uncertainty. I'm going right now to look for Gerardo Silva."

"But it's still dark out, ma'am. What can you do?"

"Tell Anselmo to stop sweeping and come with me."

The lady went into one of the darkened rooms to get her coat. The cook went out to warn Anselmo.

Some moments later the first rays of dawn appeared. A carriage came to a stop at the front door. Inside were the General, the two congressmen, and Rosalitos.

"Good-bye," the General said as he got out of the carriage.

"Good-bye, General," his companions answered.

The lady observed this scene from behind the French doors leading to the balcony. When she saw her husband get out of the carriage safe and sound, she took off her coat and returned to her bedroom.

The General opened the door to his room with a key he always carried with him, and went to bed after giving orders to Petra that no one disturb him.

We will describe what happened at the duel. It had been agreed that they would fight by sword, and until blood was shed, on a certain empty lot in the Colonia de los Arquitectos. After they arrived in two separate carriages, Rosalitos announced:

"General, I am ready to serve as your second. Here are the weapons. My colleague has no objections, either. We are ready and stand on our honor; but before the fighting begins, let me say that this duel is pointless. The person you are fighting over is not worthy of such an honor."

As the question was raised on these grounds, the contenders and their seconds entered into an earnest discussion, which the early morning chill prevented from becoming too heated.

Rosalitos told a joke about Curly that made everyone laugh hilariously, and the General and the congressman embraced each other.

That afternoon, Rosalitos would notify Julia that the General had left her. He would carry out this mission with pleasure; first of all, out of respect for the General's family, and, second, because Rosalitos was single, handsome, and rich, and as he was no more than twenty-seven years old, he could handle the consequences.

The General, who entered his house a humbled man, realized that this escapade of his golden years (in which, according to his friends, he had cut such a fine figure) had been plagued by quarrels, difficulties, and vexations, all in exchange for vulgar pleasures, a paltry return compared to the happiness of his family.